"You'd rather go t

Her mind rebelled at the notion of taking her son to some strange place, surrounded by people they didn't know. But wasn't that what she'd done anyway? Dalton Hale was little more than a stranger to them. And his house was like no place she or Logan had ever lived before.

But she felt safe there, she realized. She had no particular reason to feel that way, but she did, regardless.

"No," she said, not intending to say so aloud but not really regretting it when she heard the word slip over her tongue.

She felt his gaze on her again, a caress of scrutiny that sent a little shiver of awareness darting down her spine. He released a soft breath, as if he'd been holding it.

"I don't regret asking you to stay with me."

"I don't regret staying." She slanted a quick look toward him. "We'll have to take pains to keep it that way, won't we?"

THE LEGEND OF SMUGGLER'S CAVE

Paula Graves

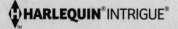

Recycling programs for this product may not exist in your area.

For my niece Melissa, who has added unexpected joy to my life in some of the most surprising ways. I love you, Missy. Now go do your homework.

ISBN-13: 978-0-373-69753-3

THE LEGEND OF SMUGGLER'S CAVE

Printed in U.S.A.

HARLEQUIN®
www.Harlequin.com

ABOUT THE AUTHOR

Alabama native Paula Graves wrote her first book, a mystery starring herself and her neighborhood friends, at the age of six. A voracious reader, Paula loves books that pair tantalizing mystery with compelling romance. When she's not reading or writing, she works as a creative director for a Birmingham advertising agency and spends time with her family and friends. She is a member of Southern Magic Romance Writers, Heart of Dixie Romance Writers and Romance Writers of America.

Paula invites readers to visit her website, www.paulagraves.com.

Books by Paula Graves

HARLEQUIN INTRIGUE

926—FORBIDDEN TERRITORY
998—FORBIDDEN TEMPTATION
1046—FORBIDDEN TOUCH
1088—COWBOY ALIBI
1183—CASE FILE: CANYON CREEK, WYOMING*
1189—CHICKASAW COUNTY CAPTIVE*
1224—ONE TOUGH MARINE*
1230—BACHELOR SHERIFF*
1272—HITCHED AND HUNTED**
1278—THE MAN FROM GOSSAMER RIDGE**
1285—COOPER VENGEANCE**
1305—MAJOR NANNY
1337—SECRET IDENTITY§
1342—SECRET HIDEOUT§
1348—SECRET AGENDA§
1366—SECRET ASSIGNMENT§
1372—SECRET KEEPER§
1378—SECRET INTENTIONS§
1428—MURDER IN THE SMOKIES‡‡
1432—THE SMOKY MOUNTAIN MIST‡‡
1438—SMOKY RIDGE CURSE‡‡
1473—BLOOD ON COPPERHEAD TRAIL‡‡
1479—THE SECRET OF CHEROKEE COVE‡‡
1486—THE LEGEND OF SMUGGLER'S CAVE‡‡

*Cooper Justice
**Cooper Justice: Cold Case Investigation
§Cooper Security
‡‡Bitterwood P.D.

CAST OF CHARACTERS

Briar Blackwood—Bitterwood's newest cop becomes the police department's next mystery when her ruthless cousin tries to use her son as leverage to find what Briar's late husband, Johnny, stole from a mountain crime lord.

Dalton Hale—The Ridge County assistant D.A. believes Briar holds the key to breaking open an ongoing investigation that could repair his professional ambitions. But will the resourceful young widow repair his broken personal life, as well?

Logan Blackwood—Briar will do anything to protect her three-year-old son.

Blake Culpepper—Briar's dangerous cousin has set his sights on controlling a criminal enterprise teetering on the brink of collapse, and there's nothing he won't do to get his way.

Doyle Massey—The Bitterwood chief of police just found a brother he never knew about, but Dalton Hale wants nothing to do with him. Can he convince the stubborn, bitter D.A. that they're on the same side?

Dana Massey—She's already lost one brother, and the newfound brother she's just discovered wants nothing to do with her. But she's not the sort of woman to give up without a fight.

Walker Nix—The Bitterwood P.D. detective is Briar Blackwood's closest friend. He's not sure she should trust Dalton Hale with her son's life...or her own.

Leanne Dawson—The pretty bookkeeper had a torrid affair with Johnny Blackwood shortly before his death. Does she know something that could break open the case?

Thurman Gowdy—The wily old cop is Briar's patrol partner and mentor. His training may mean the difference between life and death as she goes up against a band of tough, relentless opponents.

Chapter One

The front door was unlocked. Jenny never left it unlocked.

Hair rising on her neck and arms, Briar Blackwood took a careful step backward on the porch and drew her Glock 27. Not her weapon of choice; her Mossberg 835 shotgun was locked in the cabinet inside the cabin. But the Glock would do.

She stayed still for a breathless moment, listening for movement within the cabin. Was she overreacting? Maybe her aunt had fallen asleep on the sofa without locking up.

No. The break-in a month earlier had rattled Aunt Jenny's nerves. She hadn't been comfortable staying at Briar's place with Logan alone at night since. She always locked all the doors and windows the second Briar left and wouldn't even answer the door unless she knew the voice on the other side.

So why was the door unlocked now?

Everyone who mattered to Briar was behind that unlocked door. And she could stand here holding her breath, or she could go in there to see what was what.

But not through the front door.

Briar edged to the corner of the porch, making herself a harder target if someone inside started shooting. Tightening her grip on the Glock, she pulled her cell phone from her jacket pocket and dialed the cabin landline. She heard the phone ringing through the cabin walls.

No answer.

Now she knew for sure something was wrong. Aunt Jenny was a light sleeper. She never slept through a ringing phone.

Shoving her cell phone back in her pocket, Briar slid between the wood slabs of the porch railing and dropped three feet to the ground below. Stopping below the big kitchen window, she peered up at the jars of fruits and vegetables stacked in three tight rows in front of the window. The colorful jars took the place of curtains, both as a dash of brightness in the small kitchen and as a privacy screen, keeping out the unwanted gazes of strangers who might be lurking outside the mountain cabin.

They were still intact. Last time someone had broken in, they'd shattered the jars and left a huge mess in her kitchen.

What could they want? She was poor as a church mouse. Her new job as a Bitterwood police officer would do little more than pay the bills and allow her to put aside a little bit for her son Logan's college fund.

Could it be her job that had drawn the intruders to her door?

She edged her way around to the root cellar door and eased it open, wincing at the low creaks of the hinges. Six concrete steps took her down into the tightly packed cellar, where shelves full of canned goods filled one side of the room, and bins of root vegetables filled the other. She used the flashlight app on her cell phone to illuminate the narrow path between shelves and bins, but she still managed to stumble into the shelves near the stairs. With a muttered curse, she barely caught a jar of tomatoes as it started to topple off the shelf above.

Setting it right, she shined the cell-phone light up the

stairs. The door to the cabin was closed. She crept up the stairs and tried the doorknob. Locked, as expected. She eased her keys from her pocket and inserted the right one. The doorknob turned smoothly, and she carefully slipped into the hallway, shutting off the phone light.

She went very still, just listening. There was no sound at all, she realized. Not even the hum of the refrigerator or the whir of heated air blowing from the wall heater nearby.

The power must be out. Had someone cut it?

Glad for the rubber soles of her work shoes, she went silently into the living room and took a quick scan of the situation. Her eyes had begun to adjust to the low light, allowing her to see that the living room was a mess. Sofa cushions had been pulled from the sofa and ripped open, the stuffing lying all over everything. The intruders may have spared her jars of fruits and vegetables this time, but most of the contents of her refrigerator lay scattered across the floor and counters of the tiny kitchen, going to ruin.

She stepped back into the hallway, her heart pounding with equal parts adrenaline and dread.

Please, God, let Logan and Jenny be okay. Please, please, please....

The door to her own bedroom was closest. That was where Jenny slept when Briar was working a night shift, as she'd done during her stint as a dispatcher, and as she'd be doing for the first few months on the job as a police officer. But when Briar tried to push the door open, something was blocking it. She peered through the narrow space between the door and the frame and saw a pale white hand outstretched.

Jenny!

A noise in the next room down made her freeze. That was Logan's room.

Someone was moving within.

She reached through the narrow crack in the door and touched her fingertips to Jenny's wrist. Relief rattled through her when she found a strong, steady pulse.

Pulling back, she pushed to her feet and fell back on her police-academy training, so recently finished. She led with her pistol, moving as quietly and quickly as she could. The thumping sound she'd heard earlier repeated. A drawer closing, she recognized.

She touched the door and found that it wasn't latched. It swung open slowly and silently—thank God she'd oiled the hinges recently. It used to creak like crazy.

A tall dark-clad figure stood silhouetted by the faint moonlight coming through Logan's window. He had his back to her, allowing her to spare a quick glance toward the bed to reassure herself that Logan was still there, his face turned toward his pillow and his little chest rising slowly and steadily.

"Freeze—police!"

The dark silhouette whirled not toward her but toward Logan's bed.

She couldn't fire at him, not with her son so close, so she shoved the gun in her jacket pocket and ran, hitting the intruder solidly. They both bounced off the bed and hit the floor.

"Mama!" Logan's soft, frightened wail tore at Briar's heart, but she couldn't let go of the man punching and kicking at her in an attempt to escape.

He eluded her grasp and started toward the door. She scrambled up after him, tackling him as he darted into the hall.

Suddenly, strong, cruel fingers bit into her arm at the same time she was yanked back by her hair, allowing the man she'd brought down to scurry out of reach.

She grabbed the Glock from her jacket and twisted around, shoving the barrel at her captor. "Let me go!"

He dropped her with a hard shove, slamming her back into the floor. Her head hit the hardwood with a jarring thud, and for a second the whole world seemed to explode into colorful confetti.

Then her vision cleared, and she swung the Glock in a semicircle, looking for any sign of the intruders.

The front door was open, barely visible from her position on the hallway floor. She pushed to her feet, wincing at the pain in her shoulder, and edged her way into the living room.

She took a quick peek outside. There was no sound of a motor, but she thought she made out the rustle of leaves in the woods just beyond her property. Even with a three-quarter moon in the sky, she couldn't detect any movement in the gloom of the woods, just the fading rustles of the two intruders running away.

She shoved the door closed and engaged the lock, her heart pounding and her head aching.

"Mama!" Logan's wail drew her back to the hallway. Pocketing her weapon, she pulled out her cell phone and turned on the flashlight app, shining it into the darkness.

Logan stood in the middle of the hall, his blue T-shirt riding up his little round belly and his pajama pants sagging to reveal his big-boy underwear.

She ran and scooped him up, pressing her face against his little chest, breathing in the beautiful smell of sleepy little boy. "Mama's right here," she assured him, patting his back in soothing circles.

Mama's got you.

HE SHOULD HAVE known Doyle Massey would be at the hospital. The Bitterwood chief of police seemed to show up everywhere Dalton Hale went these days, like a particularly hard-to-kill weed in a flower garden. And, as luck would have it, tonight the sister was there, as well, her auburn hair, green eyes and prominent cheekbones a persistent, visible reminder of what a mess his own life had become in the last month.

Dalton had finally reached the point, however, where the sight of Doyle and Dana Massey didn't send him into a seething rage. At least, not on the outside. He was still boiling a little inside, but he set that emotion aside and entered the Maryville Mercy Hospital waiting room with his head high and his own green eyes clear and focused.

He bumped gazes with Laney Hanvey, who sat next to Massey. She was about to marry the chief, which had strained their formerly collegial relationship, but she was still the friendliest face in the room. She murmured something to her fiancé and crossed the room to meet him.

"Is something wrong?" she asked quietly.

He realized she didn't know he was there for the same reason she was. "Not on my end of things. I'm here to talk to the victim."

Her gaze narrowed. "Jenny Franklin is still undergoing tests."

"I meant the widow. The Blackwood woman." He realized, as Laney's expression darkened, that he sounded cold and officious. Not the sort of man he'd ever been, not before now. He'd been the prosecutor who went the extra mile, tried to get to know the people for whom he sought justice. He still received Christmas cards from people he'd helped. He never used to call people things like *victim* or *the widow*.

He was doing a lot of things now that he'd never done before.

"Her name is Briar," Laney said quietly. "Do you have to do this tonight?"

"Was she injured?"

"Just roughed up a little. Didn't even let the paramedics check her."

Dalton looked past Laney until his gaze snagged on the dark-haired woman sitting with a small boy sleeping in her arms. She sat apart from the others, though most of them threw concerned glances toward her now and then.

"That's her, isn't it?" He nodded toward the woman with the child.

Laney followed his gaze. "Yes. You know the police already have her statement, right? She's a cop herself. She was thorough."

That was news to him, actually. "I thought she was a dispatcher."

"She graduated from the academy back in December, and a slot opened on the police force last week, so she finally got her badge."

Laney was answering all his questions with details, he realized, because she wanted to keep him from bothering Briar Blackwood. And hell, maybe if he were in her position, he'd be doing the same. He hadn't exactly covered himself with glory over the past few weeks as he'd dealt with finding out his whole bloody life had been a lie.

Matter of fact, he'd been a complete ass about it.

"I just want to ask her a few questions about the break-in." He intentionally added a gentle tone to his voice, though he was feeling anything but gentle at the moment.

Laney's eyes narrowed again, as if she saw through the pretense. But after a moment, her expression cleared. "I'll introduce you."

He'd have preferred to approach the woman alone, away

from all her friends, but he couldn't exactly make any demands, could he? It wasn't as if she were the culprit here.

At least, not that he could prove.

He followed Laney across the waiting room floor, ignoring the watchful gazes of the others, though he did spare the slightest glance at Dana Massey, as if his eyes couldn't resist one more quick look to make sure he hadn't been mistaken about the resemblance.

No, still there, the faint but unmistakable traits that had convinced her, on the day of their first meeting, that he was the long-lost half brother she'd only recently learned about.

He dragged his gaze forward, grinding his teeth.

"Briar?"

The dark-haired woman looked up at Laney, then let her gaze slide slowly to Dalton's face, her clear gray eyes darkening with recognition. So she already knew who he was. Probably not good news, given the tumble his reputation had taken around the Bitterwood Police Department in the past few weeks.

"Mrs. Blackwood, I'd like to ask you a few questions about the break-in this evening," he said, not waiting for the unnecessary introduction.

Beside him, Laney released a soft sigh. "Briar, this is assistant county prosecutor Dalton Hale."

"I know who he is," she said quietly, still holding his gaze. "I've given a statement to the Bitterwood Police Department. Detective Nix is the lead detective." She nodded toward the dark-haired man sitting next to Dana Massey. Walker Nix. Bitterwood detective and Dana's significant other. Nix stared back at him, as if daring him to cause a ruckus.

In Briar's lap the dark-haired little boy stirred and made a low mewling noise that sounded like a puppy whining. He tightened his little arms around his mother's neck, clinging like a monkey as she rubbed his back and murmured soothing nonsense to him until he settled down.

A painful sensation wriggled in the pit of his stomach. He killed it with ruthless dispatch. "I understand that. But I have some questions about the incident that the detective may not have known to ask."

Something shifted in those gunmetal eyes, a flicker of flame warming their wintry depths. "Such as?"

Ah, he thought, *she's curious.* That was good. Curiosity was exactly the sort of trait he needed from this woman if he was going to get the answers he sought. "Such as, do you believe this most recent break-in could be related to the one that happened a few weeks ago?"

Her eyes went from molten steel to flinty ice in a split second. "What makes you think Nix wouldn't have asked such an obvious question? Do you have such a low opinion of the police?"

Dalton gave himself a mental kick. Once more he was letting his anger at Massey taint everything and everyone connected to him. Of course Nix would have asked the obvious question. "Fair enough."

Briar glanced up at Laney. Some communication moved silently between them, for Laney patted Briar's arm and walked away, leaving him alone with her.

He sat in the empty chair beside her. "You like handling things on your own. Don't you?"

She didn't answer.

"You're sitting off here by yourself, away from your friends. You sent Laney away so you could handle my questions alone."

"You seem to know something, or think you know something, about the break-in. So spill it." She kept her voice low, her hand still drawing soothing circles around her son's back.

"I know your husband died seven months ago."

"He was *murdered* seven months ago," she corrected quietly. Her voice had an oddly detached tone, making him wonder about the state of the relationship at the time of Johnny Blackwood's murder.

"You weren't a suspect?"

Her gaze flicked toward him. "I had an alibi."

"Work?" She'd still been the emergency services night-shift dispatcher at the time of Johnny's death.

She nodded. "Plenty of security video to establish my whereabouts."

"But you had a motive?"

She took a quick, sharp breath through her nose. "Is there a point to this line of questioning?"

He supposed there wasn't, other than curiosity. He knew the basics about Johnny Blackwood's goings and comings during the months leading up to his murder. It was how he'd latched on to Johnny in the first place—reading through the case notes and seeing signs of a potential connection to another case he was looking into. But the personal details in the case file were scarce, perhaps because Briar was part of the Bitterwood P.D. family. Personal matters not pertaining to the case would have been minimized and even left out to protect her privacy.

Like the state of the marriage at the time of his death. The cops would have wanted to know if there had been trouble in her relationship with her husband. And Dalton knew that on Johnny's side, at least, there had been trouble to spare.

But did his wife know what Dalton knew?

As he puzzled through how best to ask her such a delicate question, a doctor in a white jacket over green scrubs entered the waiting room. "Mrs. Franklin's family?"

Briar's whole body seemed to snap to tautness at the

sound of the doctor's voice. She stood, clutching her small son more tightly to her, and crossed to meet the doctor halfway.

Dalton trailed behind her, catching up in time to hear the doctor say, "We'll want to keep her until tomorrow because she lost consciousness, but she's not showing any continuing mental confusion, which is a very good sign. She did sustain a fracture of both bones in her lower right arm, however. We've reset the bones and applied a fiberglass cast to just above the elbow. She'll need to wear the cast for at least four weeks."

"Can I see her?" Briar asked.

"Check with the nurse at the front desk in the E.R.— she'll tell you what room she'll be in." The doctor smiled, gave Briar a comforting pat on her shoulder and left the waiting room, moving at a clip.

"Good news," Dalton murmured.

Briar turned her gaze toward him, her eyes narrowing. "You're still here."

"Yes, I am," he said, not taking offense. He knew he was making a nuisance of himself by coming here at this hour of night to bother her, but it couldn't be helped. She might hold the key to his uncertain future without even realizing it.

"I have to go check on my aunt." She turned away from him and crossed to where Laney sat, murmuring something before she handed off her son to the other woman.

Dalton watched her straighten her back and leave the waiting room with her shoulders squared and her chin up, like a soldier readied for battle. It struck him, in that brief glimpse of her steel core, that Briar Blackwood was a woman who thrived on challenges that made other people collapse.

Could that trait of hers be useful to him?

As Dalton started out the door after her, Doyle Massey rose from his chair and moved into his path. He was smiling as he did so, in that charming snake-oil salesman way of his, all teeth and beach tan and ulterior motives.

"Where are you going?" Doyle asked.

"That's none of your business." Dalton tried to take a step around him, but Doyle shifted, staying in his path.

"I don't know what you're up to or why you've suddenly taken an interest in my newest recruit, but don't drag our bad blood into it."

Dalton couldn't help smiling at the chief's choice of words. "Bad blood, huh?"

"Dana and I get that you don't want to be part of our family, and you know, we can live with that. But don't think that means we'll let you screw with our lives and the lives of people around us."

"Your faith in my integrity is touching."

"I have no faith in you at all," Doyle snapped back, dropping all pretense of friendly civility. "What brought you here tonight?"

"A case." Dalton lifted his chin, daring the chief to start a fight.

"Which case is that?"

Dalton glanced to his right as Walker Nix rose from his seat and headed for the waiting room door. Off to see after the Blackwood widow and her aunt, he guessed. Maybe take the older woman's statement.

He'd wanted to be there for that statement himself, but clearly the chief had other ideas.

"Why don't you both try being straight with each other?" Laney rose from her chair and moved to turn their tense twosome into a threesome.

They both looked at her, and she lifted her eyebrows in response.

Doyle looked back at Dalton, his eyebrows mimicking his fiancée's. "Well? What case are we talking about?"

Dalton was tempted to just leave without answering. But with so much on the line—not just his own ambitions but the safety of all the people he'd sworn justice for—he couldn't afford to let his emotions muck up the works.

"I've been trying to piece together a conspiracy case against the people we suspect were involved in the Wayne Cortland crime network," he said finally, lowering his voice by habit. "You know that Blake Culpepper has been fingered as one of the people involved."

"And you come here in the middle of the night to a hospital waiting room to ask Blake's distant cousin questions about his criminal activity?" Doyle sound unconvinced.

"Not about Culpepper." Dalton tamped down a smile at the thought that he actually knew something his know-it-all half brother didn't. "I came here to ask her questions about her late husband."

"You have questions about Johnny? Why?"

"Because odds are good he was part of Cortland's organization."

Chapter Two

Briar had never liked hospitals, even before her mother's death from breast cancer. The antiseptic smells, the dim artificial lights, the rhythms of machines that beat like the pulse of some giant predatory beast—they were alien to the life she knew, a life of fresh air, changing seasons, the loamy essence of earth and trees and the feel of wind in her hair.

In the white-sheeted hospital bed, her aunt looked like a thin, sickly child instead of a strong, wiry woman in her late fifties. Her shiny silver-streaked black hair looked dull and brittle beneath the single light shining over her bed, and when Jenny turned her tired gaze to Briar, she looked as if she'd aged a decade overnight.

The cast on her right arm was bulky and the color of old paper, not quite white, not quite yellow. "Does it hurt?" Briar asked, resting her hand on the rough-textured surface of the cast.

"Not at the moment."

There was a knock on the door behind her. Then it inched open and Walker Nix's face appeared in the opening. "Is it okay to come in?"

Briar looked at her aunt. "I think Walker wants to ask you some questions about what happened."

"Of course." Jenny flashed the detective a wan smile as he entered and came to stand at the foot of her bed.

"How're you feeling?" he asked Jenny, briefly squeezing Briar's shoulder before dropping his hand to his pocket to pull out a notebook.

"I'm not feeling much of anything at the moment," Jenny admitted, making Briar smile. "I guess you want to know what I remember."

"As much as you can."

Briar's aunt lifted her left hand to her brow. "I'd just put Logan to bed when there was a knock on the door." Jenny's gaze slanted to meet Briar's. "I know you say never to answer the door at night, but the person on the other side said he was Doyle Massey, and you know that light on the porch went out night before last."

Briar gave herself a mental kick. "I meant to put a new bulb in before I left tonight."

"You can imagine what I was thinking." Jenny reached out to Briar, clasping her hand when she offered it. "It was your second week on the police force, and here was the chief of police knocking at the door in the middle of the night...."

It had been a ruse guaranteed to get Jenny to open the door, which meant the intruders were familiar enough with her life to know it would work, Briar realized with a shudder of dismay.

"Did you get a good look at the intruders?" Nix asked.

"They wore face paint and dark camouflage. One of them had a skull cap kind of hat—black, I think. It was dark and it all happened so fast. His hair was up under the cap, so I couldn't tell you what color it was. I think his eyes were dark—they didn't really give me much time to look at them, to be honest. Just pushed me inside, turned out the lights and started throwing me around."

Anger built like a fire in the pit of Briar's gut. "Did you fight them?"

Jenny shook her head, looking stricken. "First blow, they broke my arm. Felt like they'd torn it clear off. Then I guess I hit my head on the hearth, because the next thing I remember is waking up when you came into the bedroom to check on me. I don't even know how I got there."

The intruders had probably dragged her there so they wouldn't have to step over her body while they ransacked the place, Briar thought. "The hospital has her clothes. They've bagged them up for evidence," she told Nix.

He nodded, his dark eyes reflecting the fire she felt roiling in her gut. "Miss Jenny, is there anything else you can remember? Did the men say anything when they were pushing you around?"

Jenny reached up and dashed away tears that had welled in her eyes. "I'm not sure—it was all such a blur…."

Briar squeezed her aunt's hand. "You never know what might make sense to someone else."

Jenny gave her hand a little squeeze back. "The other man said something about books."

Nix and Briar exchanged glances. "What books?" Nix asked.

"I don't know." Jenny shook her head, wincing as the motion apparently made her headache flare up. "He just said something like 'The books could be anywhere.'"

"What kind of books do you have?" Nix asked Briar curiously.

"Nothing valuable," she assured him. "Some of Logan's picture books, all my books from community college, some novels. Johnny didn't do a lot of reading for pleasure, so I don't even know if I have any of his books left. But none of them would be worth breaking into a cabin and beating up a woman for. Believe me."

Jenny's eyelids were drooping, Briar noticed, though she was trying not to show her weariness. Turning to Nix, Briar gave a little nod of her head toward the door.

"Miss Jenny, thank you for the information. I'm going to head out now and let you get some rest." Nix closed up his notebook and put it back in his pocket. "You just let me know if you remember anything else."

"I don't know how much help I've been," Jenny said with a sigh.

"You've been a big help," Briar assured her. "Now I want you to concentrate on feeling better. Okay?"

"Who's going to keep Logan for you while I'm all trussed up in this thing?" Jenny feebly lifted the heavy cast on her broken arm.

Briar hadn't had time to think that far ahead. "I'll figure it out, Aunt Jenny. You know I always do."

"I'm sorry. I shouldn't have opened the door."

As Nix headed for the door, Briar bent and kissed her aunt's furrowed brow. "You didn't do anything wrong. Don't fret yourself about it, okay?"

She waited by her aunt's bedside until the older woman had drifted back to sleep. Then she tiptoed out of the room.

Nix was waiting outside the door, leaning against the wall. "She's lucky to be alive."

"I know." Briar pushed back the springy curls that had slipped the bonds of her ponytail holder to fall in her face. She'd already had a rougher night off duty than she'd had on patrol. "What are the odds this break-in isn't related to the previous one?"

Nix fell into step with her as she started down the hallway toward the waiting room. "I don't know. We thought the last break-in was related to Dana's visit, remember?"

"The Cumberland curse," she murmured. Shortly after

Dana had made a visit to Briar's cabin, someone had broken in and trashed the place. Briar had assumed the break-in might have been an act of malice, to punish her for letting Tallie Cumberland's daughter into her home.

The people of her small community, Cherokee Cove, had come to blame the Cumberlands for almost everything that went wrong in their world. Dana Massey's mother, Tallie Cumberland, had become the target of a ruthless wealthy family after she'd accused them of stealing her child.

Dalton Hale's family, in fact.

It didn't matter that Tallie had told the truth. Subtly but unmistakably, Sutherlands and Hales had let it be known that any friend of a Cumberland was an enemy. And their influence in Bitterwood was far and wide. Nobody defied them without consequences. Tallie had left Bitterwood before the age of twenty, driven from town along with her family.

When Dana Massey had come to Bitterwood a couple of months ago, looking so much like her mother, a new round of Cumberland-curse fever had commenced. At the time of the last break-in, Briar and Nix had assumed one of her Cherokee Cove neighbors had been leaving her a message about mixing with Cumberlands.

Now she wasn't so sure.

"Is Dalton Hale still here?" she asked Nix.

"He was still in the waiting room when I left."

Great, she thought. *Just great.*

What the hell did he want with her, anyway? Why had he been asking questions about Johnny's murder? That mystery had been languishing in cold-case territory for months now.

Why was the Ridge County prosecutor's office suddenly interested in the murder again?

DALTON HALE HAD never seen himself as an angry man. Passionate, yes. Forceful in the pursuit of justice. But not one who possessed the kind of bitter rage that destroyed the lives and families of those who passed through his world.

But he was angry now. Fury burned in his gut like acid, eating away at every vestige of the man he'd once believed himself to be. It had poisoned his relationship with his father and grandfather until he'd found himself struggling to speak to them with any semblance of civility. It had ripped holes in the solid foundation of his career, taking him overnight from golden boy to uncertain risk in the eyes of the men and women who could make or break his future.

And for what? For a lie told years ago and a truth buried for over three decades. The vindication of a woman long dead and the total destruction of a man whose name had once meant something, not just here in Tennessee but all the way to the steps of the United States Capitol.

In a world where very little in life was fair, Dalton had spent his own life trying to even the odds for people without power or privilege.

People like the woman who had given birth to him.

And now he was angry at her, too. For having existed. For having come back here nearly fifteen years ago for one last look at the son she'd left behind. For becoming, with her husband, a victim of his grandfather's steely will and his father's emotional weakness.

And for giving birth to another son and a daughter who had invaded his well-planned world and asked inconvenient questions about a truth that should have remained buried.

They had made him into a man he didn't recognize anymore.

And he was angry at himself, most of all, for letting them.

Maybe if he'd been brought up by earthy, straight-talking mountain folk like his birth mother, he could have vented all this rage in one rip-roaring, glass-smashing, fist-flying explosion. Gone on a tear and let the fury have reign. Got it out of his system and been done with it.

But he'd been raised by Nina Hale, not Tallie Cumberland. And Hales didn't throw angry fits. They kept their emotions under control, functioning on reason and behaving at all times with civility and good manners.

Except when they were killing inconvenient people, he reminded himself as he faced his half brother with clenched fists and fought the urge to take a swing.

"What evidence do you have to support your theory about Johnny Blackwood?" Doyle's calm tone was deceptive. Dalton didn't miss the dangerous gleam of anger in the chief's green eyes, eyes so like his own that he'd all but given up hoping the past couple of months had all been one nightmarish mistake.

"I'm not prepared to try my case before you, chief."

"In other words, you're talking out your—"

Laney put her hand on Doyle's arm, stopping him midsentence. "Dalton's been looking into the Wayne Cortland case," she told her fiancé. "He's been trying to unravel the Tennessee side of the organization, see if he can build criminal cases against everyone involved."

Doyle's expression took on a slight grudging hint of admiration that caught Dalton by surprise. Even worse, he felt an answering flutter of something that might be satisfaction deep in the pit of his gut, as if the chief's approval actually mattered. He beat back the sensation with ruthless determination.

"I have to confess, I don't know a lot about Johnny Blackwood," Doyle said in a less confrontational tone. "I know he was murdered several months ago, and the case went cold pretty quickly."

"It's not his murder that interests me," Dalton answered before he remembered he didn't want to share any information with the chief. He sighed, knowing what he'd said would only make Massey more, not less, interested in Johnny Blackwood's possible connection to Cortland.

Fortunately, Briar Blackwood chose that moment to return to the waiting room. She looked tired and angry, her black curls spilling into her face from her untidy ponytail as she strode into the room. Her storm-cloud eyes locked with his, and she gave a curt backward nod of her head, a silent invitation to join her outside. She murmured something to Nix and then walked out of the waiting room again.

"I have to go," Dalton murmured, already moving toward the door.

"Be careful. She's tougher than she looks." Doyle's words sounded more like a taunt than a warning.

His back stiffening, Dalton left the waiting room and looked up and down the corridor for the Blackwood woman.

She stood at the window at the far end of the hall, her back to him. She had a neat, slim figure accentuated by snug jeans and a curve-hugging long-sleeved T-shirt. The messy ponytail had almost given up, gathering only a small clump of curls at the back of her neck while the rest of her hair spilled free across her shoulders. As he walked toward her, she reached back and pulled the elastic band free, letting the rest of her hair loose to tangle and coil around her neck.

An unexpected tug in his groin caught Dalton by surprise. His steps faltered before he caught himself.

Not an option, Hale. Not even close to an option.

Unfortunately, the more he tried not to think about Briar
Blackwood as a woman, the more of her feminine features
he noticed. Like the perfect size of her breasts, neither too
large nor too small for her compact frame. Or the flare of
her hips and curvy contours of her bottom.

She had a fine face, too—more interesting than con-
ventionally pretty, with lightly tanned skin splashed with
small cinnamon freckles and large black-fringed eyes cur-
rently the color of antique pewter.

Fire flashed in those gray eyes as she turned to look at
him. "Mr. Hale, I don't know what you think you know
about my husband or his murder, but if you think it's a way
to get back at your brother and sister—"

"Don't call them that."

Her dark eyebrows notched slightly upward. "You don't
get to tell me what to do. I don't sugarcoat the truth. You
and the chief share a mother. You don't have to like it. I
don't reckon he likes it much himself, but there you are
anyway. And if you're messing around in my life because
you think it'll piss off your brother, you can just move
along and find somebody else to use. I won't be party to it."

He wanted to be angry at her for her bluntness, but in
truth, he found it something of a relief. Everybody else he
knew, friends and colleagues he'd known for years, seemed
to walk around on eggshells around him, as if they feared
speaking plainly about the train wreck his life had become.
He might not like what Briar Blackwood had to say, but at
least she was saying it aloud and without apology.

"Understood," he said with similar bluntness. "But my
interest in your husband's murder has nothing to do with
Massey."

"Then why are you suddenly interested in what happened to Johnny?"

He studied her, wondering if her straightforward style

and "call a spade a spade" philosophy extended to her own life. "Why aren't you *more* interested, Mrs. Blackwood?"

His question hit the mark. He saw her eyes widen slightly, and her pink lips flattened with annoyance. "What makes you think I'm not?"

"Most people who lose a loved one to murder don't move on with their lives so easily."

The fire returned to those gunmetal eyes. "What would you have me do? Bury myself with him? Turn the cabin into a shrine and worship his memory? I have a small son. I have bills to pay and debts to honor. I don't have time to haunt the police station begging them to solve his case. I was there for the whole thing. I knew how hard they tried to follow leads. But there weren't any leads to follow. Not here in Ridge County."

"Where, then, if not here in Ridge County?" he asked softly.

Up flickered those eyes again, changing tone with quicksilver speed. Now they were hard edged and cold as hoarfrost. "What made you come to Maryville at this time of night to ask me questions about my husband? Why tonight, smack in the middle of all this uproar?"

She wasn't going to tell him what he needed to know, he saw, unless he gave her something in return. The chief was right—she *was* tougher than she looked. But how much could he tell her without driving her further away?

"I'm investigating the Wayne Cortland crime organization. I assume, as a police officer, you have at least a passing knowledge of the case."

She nodded quickly. "I do."

Much of the information he'd gathered over the past few months was highly confidential, but he had a feeling he wouldn't get far with this woman if he didn't cough up a little new information. But the newest revelation of his ongoing investigation, the lead that had brought him to Maryville Mercy Hospital in the middle of the night, was something he didn't think Johnny Blackwood's widow wanted to hear.

"I'm trying to connect the dots between Cortland and some of the Tennessee groups that may have been working for him."

"I know. My cousin Blake is part of the Blue Ridge Infantry. Tennessee division." She spoke in a dry, humorless drawl liberally spiced with disdain. Clearly not a fan of either her cousin or his pretense of patriotism. Good. That made his work here marginally less difficult.

But only marginally.

He paused a moment to size her up again, telling himself it wasn't an excuse to appreciate once more her tempting curves. But his body's heated reaction demolished that lie in a few accelerated heartbeats.

He forced his focus back to the problem of her husband's potential involvement in Cortland's organization. "How much did you know about your husband's job?"

She hadn't been expecting that question, he saw. Her brows furrowed and she cocked her head slightly to one side, countering with a question of her own. "What do *you* know about my husband's job?"

"He was a driver with Davenport Trucking."

Her eyes narrowed. "And because Wayne Cortland was trying to take control of Davenport Trucking through a proxy, you're wondering if Johnny might have been on Cortland's payroll."

"Yes," he answered, though it wasn't the entire truth. He hadn't made the connection between Johnny and Cortland because of Davenport Trucking, but if she bought that reason for his questions, he'd go with it.

"That's thin gruel," she said with a shake of her head.

"There are dozens of people driving trucks for Davenport Trucking. You have another reason for targeting Johnny."

"He was murdered."

"And you think it's connected to Cortland because…?"

She wasn't going to be mollified by half truths, he saw with dismay. Not only was she tougher than she looked; she was smarter than he'd reckoned.

Still, he gave it one more shot, not so much out of concern for her feelings as from his own bone-deep weariness of scandal and acts of betrayal. "Can you accept that I have my reasons and I'm not inclined to share them?"

The look she gave him was uncomfortably penetrating. He felt himself closing up in defense, not ready to have her poking around in his brain.

She turned suddenly and started walking away.

"Wait." He trailed after her.

She stopped and whirled around so quickly he almost barreled into her. "I want the truth. I don't need you to protect my feelings or try to handle me. If you can't play fair, you can count me out of your game."

"It's not a game."

"What drew your attention to my late husband? What makes you think he's connected to Wayne Cortland?"

There was steel in her voice but also a hint of a tremor, as if she knew whatever he had to say would be bad. So she hadn't been naive about Johnny Blackwood's personal failings, he thought. It wouldn't make the truth any less sordid, but she might be less injured by the blow.

"I'll make it easier for you," she said quietly, her gaze dropping to the collar of his shirt. "The day Johnny's body showed up on Smoky Ridge, I'd spoken to a lawyer about filing for divorce."

The words were spoken flatly, but Dalton didn't miss the

tremble of vulnerability that underlay them. Not a broken heart, he assessed silently, but a deeply shattered pride.

"I didn't know. I'm sorry."

She gave an impatient toss of her dark curls. "Just tell me why you think Johnny was involved with Cortland."

"Because he was involved with Cortland's secretary," Dalton answered. "They were having an affair. And she thinks he was using her to get closer to Wayne Cortland."

Chapter Three

Briar didn't flinch. She didn't tremble or cry or do anything that Dalton Hale was clearly bracing himself to deal with as he lowered the boom.

But inside she died a little, another tiny piece of herself ripping away to join the other little scraps of soul shrapnel that had come unmoored during the slow unraveling of her marriage.

"How long?" she asked, pleased at the uninflected tone of her voice.

"She says about three months."

That was about right, she thought, remembering the growing distance between Johnny and her in the months before his murder. In fact, she'd long suspected he might have been unfaithful during her early pregnancy, when her normally sturdy body had betrayed her with dizzy spells and five months of near-constant nausea before she'd regained her strength for the last four months.

Johnny had liked the idea of having a baby, but the process had left him feeling peevish and neglected. As if the whole thing should have been about him and not the baby she was desperately trying to carry to a healthy birth.

In fact, he'd reacted like an overgrown baby himself. It had marked the beginning of the long, tortuous end of their twelve-year romance.

"Mrs. Blackwood?"

She realized she hadn't responded to him, hadn't even moved a muscle, her body and mind focused inward to her own unexpected pain. She gathered the tatters of her wits to ask, "What makes her think he was using her to get to Cortland?"

"Do you really want that much detail?" he asked, not unkindly.

She supposed not. At least, not right now, when she was still processing another ugly piece of truth about the only man she'd ever loved. "Did she offer any proof other than her own feelings?" The question came out with a hint of cold disdain. Not an attractive sound, but she couldn't unsay it.

"I'm not at liberty—"

"Get back to me when you are." She turned and started walking away once more, this time not stopping when he called her name.

She entered the waiting room, where only Nix and Logan remained. Logan lay curled up in the chair beside Nix, fast asleep.

"Everybody else had to go," Nix said quietly, rising as he spotted her. "Work comes bright and early in the morning."

"For you, too," she said with a faint smile, hoping her inner turmoil wasn't showing. Nix was the closest thing she had to a brother, and if he thought for a moment that Dalton Hale had upset her, he might go looking to mete out a little Smoky Mountain justice on her behalf.

"This *is* my work."

He opened his arms and she slipped into his brotherly embrace, glad that his deepening relationship with the chief's sister hadn't changed the warmth of their own long-standing friendship. Right now she needed a friend in her corner, someone who'd back her up without asking any hard questions. "Aunt Jenny's probably not going to be up for any more questions tonight. You can go home and get some sleep."

He rubbed her back. "You and Logan are coming home with me."

She looked up at him. "Dana's okay with that?"

"She's making up the sofa bed as we speak."

"Don't screw up and let that one go," she said. "I like her."

"Yeah, I kind of like her, too," Nix murmured.

As she started to pull away from his embrace, movement in the doorway caught her eye. Dalton Hale stood there, watching her and Nix through narrowed eyes. She let go of Nix and turned to face him, lifting her chin. "Later, Mr. Hale."

He gave a short nod and walked away.

"You sure he's not giving you trouble?"

"No trouble," she lied, turning to ease her sleeping son out of the chair and into her arms.

DALTON TRIED TO stretch his legs, but the cab of the Chevy S-10 pickup truck was too small to allow for much motion. He'd wanted to buy a big, spacious luxury car—he had money, damn it, and it wasn't a sin to spend it on comfort sometimes. But his campaign manager, Bill Murphy, had pointed out that he was running for office in a county where many people still fed themselves and their families with wild game and the fruits of their homestead gardens. An American-made pickup truck said Dalton was one of them, just another homegrown Smoky Mountain boy. The smaller, more fuel-efficient S-10 said he was environmentally conscious and a protector of the land they all loved.

But the Infiniti M35 he'd wanted to buy instead of the

S-10 would have said he was a tall man with a good income who could afford not to have cramps in his legs to appear as if he were something he wasn't.

Serving the people of his county shouldn't have been so damned hard. Whatever people like Doyle Massey and Briar Blackwood thought, his motives for wanting the job of head county prosecutor weren't entirely self-serving. He supposed it might be seen as a stepping-stone to state office and maybe national office one day, but if that were his only reason for wanting the job, he would have given up a long time ago. He wasn't a politician by nature. He supposed, in a sense, that trait was one he and Briar Blackwood shared in common.

Sugarcoating things had never come naturally to him.

Her house was dark and quiet. She wasn't there, of course; she worked the five-to-midnight shift at the police station—rookie hours, his clerk had called it with a laugh when he'd asked the man to learn her work hours.

Her absence was why he had come here at night to keep watch over her cabin, to see if the people who'd broken in the night before were of a mind to give it another try. He wasn't even sure she was staying here tonight; she'd stayed the previous night with Walker Nix at his Cherokee Cove cabin about a mile up the mountain. He assumed, though he couldn't know for sure, that Dana Massey had stayed there, as well, marking her territory.

That's unfair, a small voice in the back of his head admonished him. His mother's voice, he recognized—not the troubled girl who'd apparently given birth to him but the sweet-natured, softhearted woman named Nina Hale who'd raised him from infancy. *She* was his mother. Tallie Cumberland was an inconvenient fact of biology.

He hadn't talked to his mother in a couple of days. He needed to remedy that fact, because of all the people involved in the Tallie Cumberland scandal, she was the most fragile and innocent of all. She'd lost as much as Dalton had—her husband and father were in jail, looking at spending years behind bars, and she'd learned that the son she'd loved even before his birth had died in his hospital bassinet thirty-seven years ago.

He checked his watch. Only a little after nine. She'd probably be awake still, all alone in that big rambling house in Edgewood. He pulled out his cell phone and hit the speed dial for her number.

His mother answered on the second ring. "Dalton?"

"Hi, Mom."

"I've been meaning to call you all day," she said, her voice soft with badly veiled anxiety. "Your father's lawyer called this morning. He wants me to talk to Paul about taking the plea deal. Your father doesn't want to do it. You know how he can be when he sets his mind on something."

Like covering up a fifteen-year-old murder and taking potshots at a woman asking inconvenient questions, he thought. He'd never speak those thoughts aloud, of course. He loved his mother dearly, but she was no Briar Blackwood, able to take emotional body blows without batting an eye.

"I know you want him out of prison as early as possible," he said gently. "But I respect that he feels the need to pay for what he did."

"He was just trying to protect us," she said softly. "You know that's all he cared about. Tell me you know that, Dalton."

"I know that," he said, and hoped she didn't hear the doubt.

"Please talk to him. He won't let me visit him at the jail, but he'll talk to you. I know he really wants to talk to you."

Guilt sliced another piece out of his conscience. He

hadn't gone to see his father or his grandfather in a month, ever since the truth about what they'd done had finally gotten past his denial. Outrage at Doyle and Dana Massey destroying his family hadn't gone away; he'd just added fury at his father and grandfather to the toxic mix.

It wasn't healthy, feeling so angry all the time. He just hadn't yet figured out how to let go of the anger. He was beginning to wonder if he ever would.

"I'll think about it," he said, because he didn't think he could sell a lie on that particular topic, not even to his mother, who wanted to believe they could somehow patch up their shattered lives and move forward as if none of it had ever happened.

"I wouldn't mind seeing you soon, too," she added softly.

"I'll come by soon," he promised. "We'll have dinner."

"I'll make shrimp creole. Your favorite."

It hadn't been his favorite since he was eight years old and discovered the joy of Italian-sausage pizza, but he kept that fact to himself. "Can't wait."

"I love you, Dalton."

He closed his eyes, swallowing the ache in his throat. "Love you, too, Mom. I'll call you tomorrow and we'll figure out when I can make it for dinner." He slid his phone back in his pocket and settled down to watch Briar Blackwood's darkened cabin.

BY THE TIME her patrol shift ended at midnight, Briar had begun to wish she'd taken up the chief's offer of a night off to recover from the previous evening's excitement. Despite the recent rise in crime in the county, the Bitterwood P.D. night shift wasn't exactly a date with danger.

She'd answered exactly two calls during her seven-hour shift, and one of them had been a false alarm. The other had been a car crash on Old Purgatory Road near the bridge, but even that had turned out to be more paperwork than a daring rescue. Two patrons at Smoky Joe's Tavern had tried to turn out of the parking lot at the same time, crashing fenders. Neither had registered as high as .08 on the Breathalyzer, so she'd written up a report and left it to them to sort out the insurance issues.

When she dropped by Nix's cabin to pick up her son and the bag of clothes she'd packed for the overnight stay, Nix was waiting up for her. "You can stay here another night," he said when he opened the door for her.

"No, I can't." She squeezed his arm and smiled. "Got to get back on the horse again."

"A cabin break-in isn't exactly the same thing as getting tossed from a pony. Plus, you'll have to wake up the little man."

"Too late to worry about that," she murmured as she heard her son calling her name from down the hall. She followed the sound to the spare room, where Nix had set up the sofa bed for Logan, piling pillows around him to keep him from rolling too close to the edge. Logan looked sleepy and cranky, but the watery smile he flashed when he caught sight of her face made her heart melt into a sticky little pool of motherly love in the center of her chest. "Mama."

"You ready to sleep in your own bed tonight?" She plucked him from the tangle of sheets and buried her nose in his neck, reveling in the soft baby smell of him.

"Yep," he answered with an exaggerated nod that banged his little forehead against her chin. "Ow!" He giggled as he rubbed his forehead.

"Watch where you put that noggin, mister," she answered with a laugh of her own, pressing a kiss against his fingers. "Let's go home, okay?"

"I'll get his things." Nix picked up the scattered toys she'd packed for Logan while she carried him out to the front room. Nix carried the two small backpacks for her and put them in the front seat of the Jeep while she strapped Logan into his car seat in the back.

"If you decide you'd rather come back here, no matter what time it is, you pack up the little fellow and come on back. I'll keep the sofa bed ready." Nix reached through the open back door and gave Logan a head ruffle. Logan grinned up at him and patted his curls back down.

"I'll keep that in mind," she said, although nothing short of a full-on assault was going to drive her out of her own house. She wasn't going to play the damsel in distress, not even for someone like Nix, who had only her best interests at heart.

She'd made too many decisions in her life already based on what other people wanted her to do. She wasn't going to ignore her own instincts any longer.

Still, her steely resolve took a hit when Logan's sleepy voice piped up from the backseat as she turned onto the winding road to her cabin. "Mama, are the mean men gonna be there tonight? I don't like them."

She put the brakes on, slowing the Jeep to a standstill in the middle of the deserted road. "I don't like them either," she admitted, beginning to question her motives for taking her son back to the cabin so soon after the break-in. Was she willfully putting him in danger just to bolster her own desire to stand on her own two feet?

But she couldn't tuck her tail and run away from their home. It was one of the few things she could call her own in the whole world. Her great-grandfather had built the cabin over a hundred years ago with wood he'd chopped himself and the sweat of his own brow. Her grandfather had added to it over the years—indoor plumbing, extra rooms as the family had expanded. When he had died, he'd left the place to Briar's mother, who'd deeded it to Briar as a wedding gift.

It was one of the few things she had left now of her mother. That cabin and twenty-four years of good memories.

She couldn't let fear drive her away from that legacy. For her own sake and especially for Logan's.

"I won't let the bad men scare you anymore," she said firmly, hoping she was telling the truth. Because as much as she'd tried to hide it the night before at the hospital, Dalton Hale's words had weighed heavily on her. Not the thought of Johnny's infidelity—she may have been dismayed by the information, but she hadn't been surprised. But the idea that he might have gotten himself tangled up in Wayne Cortland's criminal activities—that was the notion that had nagged her every waking hour since Hale first brought up the subject.

Johnny hadn't turned out to be the strong, solid man of honor she'd thought he would be. They'd married too young, she supposed, right out of high school. They'd started trying to have a family before either of them had reached their twenties, and the lack of success for the first few years had been an unexpected strain on their bond.

She'd given up before Johnny had, figuring a child of her own just wasn't going to happen, but he'd seen the failure as a personal affront, a challenge to his masculinity. His inability to get her pregnant had turned out to be one of those moments in life where adversity led to unpleasant revelations about a person's character.

She hadn't been happy with what she'd seen in Johnny during those months when he'd fought against the tide of reality. She hadn't realized how much his sense of self had been tangled up with his notion of sexual virility, maybe because she'd made him wait until marriage before they slept together. She'd seen his patience and willingness to deny himself for her as a sign of his strength.

She'd begun to wonder, as he grew angrier and more resentful with each negative pregnancy test, if she'd read him right. What if he hadn't denied himself at all? What if he'd been sleeping with other girls the whole time she was making him wait?

Then, almost as soon as they stopped trying, she'd gotten pregnant with Logan, and for a while Johnny had seemed to be his former self: happy, good-natured and loving. Until the nausea had started, and the doctor had started warning her about the possibility of not carrying the pregnancy to term.

"Mama?"

Logan's voice held a hint of worry, making her realize how long she'd been sitting still in the middle of the road, trying to make a decision.

They were almost home. And it *was* home, after all. Two invasions of her sanctuary made her only that much more determined to reclaim its sense of peace and safety.

"We're almost home," she said firmly, shifting the rear-view mirror until she could see her son's sleepy face. He met her gaze in the mirror and grinned, melting her heart all over again.

She reached the cabin within a couple of minutes and parked in the gravel drive that ended at the utility shed at the side of the house. She paused for a moment, taking a thorough look around for any sign of intruders. But the night was dark, the moon fully obscured by lowering clouds that promised rain by morning. She still hadn't changed the front-porch light bulb, she realized with dismay. The only light that pierced the gloom was from the

Jeep's headlights, their narrow beams ending in twin circles on the flat face of the shed wall.

Don't borrow trouble, Briar Rose. The voice in her head was her mother's, from back when she'd been as strong and immovable as the rocky face of Hangman's Bald near the top of Smoky Ridge. *Don't borrow trouble—it'll come in its own sweet time, and more than soon enough.*

She cut the Jeep's engine and walked around to the passenger side to get Logan out of his seat. He lifted his arms with eagerness, despite his sleepy yawn, and she unlatched him as quickly as she could, wanting to get inside the cabin before the Jeep's headlight delay ran out.

She had just pulled him free of the car-seat belts when the headlights extinguished, plunging them into inky darkness.

Without the moon and the stars overhead, the darkness was nearly complete. The town center lay two miles to the south; her closest neighbor was a half mile up the mountain, invisible to her through the thicket of evergreens and hardwoods that grew between them.

Tucking Logan more firmly against her side, she reached in her pocket for her cell phone. Her fingers had just brushed against the smooth casing of the phone when she heard a crunch of gravel just behind her.

She let go of the phone and brought her hand up to the pancake holster she'd clipped behind her back before leaving work. But she didn't reach it before hands clawed at her face, jerking her head back until it slammed against a solid wall of heat. She heard Logan's cry and felt him being pulled from her grasp.

Clutching him more tightly, she tried to get her hand between the body that held her captive and the Glock nestled in the small of her back, but her captor's grasp was brutally strong. His fingers dug into her throat, cutting off her air for a long, scary moment.

Then the air shattered with the unmistakable crack of rifle fire, and the world around her turned upside down.

Chapter Four

The rifle kicked in Dalton's hands, nearly knocking him from his feet, but he tightened his grip and fired another warning shot into the ground, his pulse stuttering in his ears like a snare drum.

He'd had little hope that his desperate intervention would work, but to his relief, the two figures tugging at Briar Blackwood dived for cover at the second bark of the Remington.

The darkness of the night was near total, but he'd been dozing in the car for hours, his eyes adjusting to the gloom enough for him to make out the shadowy shapes of the two men escaping into the woods. Definitely both men—he had quickly discerned that fact as soon as he'd seen them gliding out of the woods in the wake of Briar's arrival.

He'd had no time to warn her, only enough time to unstrap the Remington 700 rifle that hung on a rack in the back window of the S-10's cab, another gift from his campaign manager. He knew enough about rifles to check that it was loaded and to point the barrel where it would make a loud noise but have no chance of causing injury, but in truth, he was damned lucky his ruse had worked, and he was praying like crazy as he raced toward Briar's still figure on the ground by the Jeep that the men didn't figure out he'd been bluffing.

She stirred as he came closer, putting her son between her body and the Jeep as she rose to her knees and turned a pistol toward him.

"Don't shoot! It's Dalton Hale."

She held her shooting stance for a heart-stopping moment while he froze in place. Fear flooded him, roared in his ears like a storm-tossed sea and made his hands shake as he held the rifle away in a show of surrender.

"Cover me until we reach the cabin," she rasped, shoving her weapon behind her back and turning to scoop up her son.

He hurried behind her, keeping his eyes on the woods, looking for any sign of the intruders returning, but the gloom was absolute. He heard no sounds of movement in the underbrush, however, as they hurried up the cabin steps. With a rattle of keys, Briar unlocked the door one-handed and shoved her way inside, growling for him to hurry and come in behind her.

Once he was inside, she turned the deadbolt and slumped hard against the front door, her chest rising and falling in quick, harsh gasps.

"Are you okay?" he asked, setting the rifle aside and reaching for the little boy, who was wobbling precariously in her faltering grasp.

She tried to pull her son away from him, but her knees buckled, and he grabbed the boy quickly, keeping him from falling. With alarm, he watched her slide to a sitting position in front of the door, her breath labored.

"Mama!" The child started crying, wriggling against Dalton's grasp.

"It's okay, little man. Your mama's going to be okay." He lowered the boy to the floor, and he raced away on stubby little legs, throwing himself at his mother.

She lifted her arms and hugged him close, her face

buried in his neck. "Call 911," she said, her voice muffled against her son's body.

Pulling out his cell phone, he reached for the light switch on the wall by the door. Golden light flooded the front room, making him squint as he punched in the numbers and crouched in front of Briar. A female voice came through the phone speaker. "911. What's your emergency?"

He summarized the situation quickly, putting his hand on Briar's shoulder. "I can't tell if she's injured—"

"I'm okay." Briar pulled her face away from her son's neck and met Dalton's gaze. She was pale, and her eyes were red-rimmed and damp, but her voice sounded a little less tortured, and color was coming back into her cheeks. "Tell her to call Walker Nix."

Dalton gave the instruction. "Do you want paramedics?" he asked.

Briar held her crying son away from her, looking him over for injuries. "Logan, are you okay? Do you have any boo-boos?"

"Mama!" he wailed, tightening his grip on her neck like a baby monkey.

She hugged him close and looked up at Dalton. "I think we're both okay. No paramedics."

He wasn't so sure. Dark bruises had begun to form along the curve of her throat. "You're injured," he murmured, reaching out to touch the purple spots before he realized what he was doing.

She stared up at him with wide stormy eyes, a dark flush spreading up her neck into her cheeks. "I'm fine," she said again, forcing her gaze back to her son's tearstained face. "Just get Nix here."

"Just get the police here," Dalton told the dispatcher. "I'm going to hang up now." He pocketed the phone and tried not to tumble backward out of his crouch. His knees were starting to feel like jelly.

"Can you help me up?" She reached out one hand.

He took her hand and pushed to his feet. Her fingers tightened around his as he helped her up, and she didn't let go right away, as if afraid that she might topple over again if she let go of his grasp. She had a warm, firm grip, even in her present distress, he noticed. She apparently came from what his grandfather would have called "hardy stock," for already she looked close to full recovery, save for the mottled contusions on her throat.

"Did you hit either of them?" she asked, rocking slightly from side to side as she rubbed her whimpering son's back.

He shook his head. "Didn't aim for them. I'm not a great shot, and I wasn't going to risk hitting you or the kid."

"Logan," she said with a hint of a smile. "His name is Logan."

The little boy had settled down to a series of soft hitching sniffles. "Can I get something for him?" Dalton asked, trying to remember what he'd found comforting as a little boy. "A cookie or a toy or something?"

"There's ice cream in the freezer. Strawberry—it's his favorite."

Dalton headed for the kitchen. He noticed, in passing, that she'd cleaned the place up sometime between the night before and now. Even the torn sofa cushions had been mended.

As he reached for the refrigerator's freezer compartment, Briar said, "No, not that one. The one in the corner."

He spotted a chest freezer nearby and pulled open the top. Inside, instead of the brand-name carton he was expecting, he found a large plastic tub labeled Strawberry Ice Cream in neat, clear handwriting. He pulled out the tub, uncovering what looked to be stacks and stacks of vacuum-packed cuts of some sort of meat. Looking closer, he saw that, like the ice cream, they were labeled in the same strong handwriting. Venison Shoulder, read one of the packages, with a date—December of the previous year—inscribed below. Another nearby contained pork—wild pig, to be exact—apparently put in the freezer only four weeks ago.

He closed the freezer and set the container of ice cream on the small kitchen table. "Hey, Logan, how about some ice cream?"

The little clinging monkey turned his tearstained face toward Dalton, his big gray eyes wide with a mixture of caution and curiosity.

Dalton tried again. "Ice cream, Logan. You want some?"

Logan looked up at his mother as if to seek her permission. She lowered him to the floor. "It's okay," she said. "You can have some."

Logan crossed the distance to the kitchen with small cautious steps, still watching Dalton with a healthy dose of distrust.

But when Dalton plopped a hearty scoop of homemade strawberry ice cream into the bowl in front of his chair, he climbed up and grabbed the spoon, ready to dig in. By the time Dalton put away the ice-cream container and turned back to the kitchen, Logan was half-bathed in the sticky sweet stuff.

His mother stood at one of the front windows, peering out through a narrow gap in the curtains.

"Do you see anything?" Dalton asked, walking toward her.

She let the curtains fall closed and turned to look at him. "It's dark out."

Not quite the question he'd asked, but he let it go. "How's your throat?"

"Why are you here?"

Yeah, he'd figured that question would occur to her sooner or later. "I don't suppose you'd buy it if I said I was just driving by?"

Her dark eyebrows twitched in reply.

"I was staking out the place. In case the intruders returned."

The tiniest hint of a smile curved one corner of her mouth. "And what did you plan to do if they did?"

"Call the cops."

She nodded toward the Remington 700 propped by the door. "Where'd you get the rifle?"

"It's mine."

"You hunt a lot, do you?"

He took a stab at changing the subject. "Somebody around here does. Freezer's full of game."

"I bag as much as I can during the hunting seasons. We'll live off that meat for the rest of the year." She waved her hand toward the rifle. "May I?"

He nodded, and she picked up the weapon, first checking for ammunition. "I heard two rounds. Where did you aim?"

"At the ground."

She looked up at him. "You have the rest of your ammo on you?"

He didn't know if there was any other ammunition for the rifle at all, he realized. He'd been lucky it had been loaded—he wasn't sure what he'd have done if he'd pulled the trigger and nothing had happened.

"Have you ever shot this rifle before?" She sounded as if she knew the answer.

"No."

"Why do you have it, then?"

"Emergencies," he answered, the truth too humiliating to admit.

From the look on her face, she saw through his answer anyway. She set the empty rifle against the wall. "If you'd like shooting lessons, I can help you out with that."

"For a fee?"

Her gaze snapped up to meet his. "You saved us tonight. I reckon I could let you have a lesson for free." Her voice tightened. "One, at least."

Great. He'd insulted her. "I didn't mean—"

"What do you think you're going to find here?" She leaned her back against the front wall and crossed her arms, looking at him through narrowed eyes. "Or maybe you're here because those men were working for you?"

He stared at her a moment, wondering if she was joking. The look on her face suggested otherwise. "You think I would put you and your son at risk? For what possible reason?"

"To play hero? To worm your way into my life so you could use me for whatever it is you're up to."

"What do you think I'm up to?"

She shrugged. "Hell if I know. Maybe you just want to punish your brother for existing."

He wouldn't mind knocking the smug smile off Doyle's face now and then, but he wouldn't use someone else to do it. He'd knock it off himself.

"I told you the truth last night at the hospital. I think your husband's involvement with Wayne Cortland may have gone beyond sleeping with the man's bookkeeper. I even think his murder wasn't as random as the police believe."

She was silent for a long moment, as if letting that thought sink in. Finally, she pushed herself away from the wall, rubbing her eyes with both hands. "What do you want from me? What do you think I can give you?"

It was a good question, and until just a few minutes ago, he'd have said all he wanted was a few minutes of her time, a chance to pick her brain for anything in her husband's last few months of life that might offer a new lead in the Cortland case. But two attacks on the woman in a row went far beyond coincidence. Apparently he wasn't the only person who thought Briar Blackwood could aid in the investigation, and unlike Dalton, the others didn't care who got hurt in the process.

"I think the more pressing question is, why did someone break into your house last night? And why did someone attack you again tonight?"

The sound of a truck engine began to filter through from outside the cabin, and a moment later, headlights flashed through the window, bouncing off the walls. Briar turned to the window. "It's Nix and Dana."

Dalton's heart sank. Dana. Of course she'd be with Nix. They were practically inseparable these days. Walker Nix was one of the reasons she'd decided to stick around Bitterwood instead of heading back to Atlanta.

"If you want to go without seeing your sister," Briar said quietly, "you can always go out the back."

Was his dismay so obvious? "I'm not sneaking out like a criminal."

She shrugged and opened the door at the first sound of footsteps on the front porch. Dana Massey entered first, her eyes widening a notch at the sight of Dalton. Walker Nix followed on her heels, the look he shot at Dalton tinged less with surprise and more with suspicion.

"What are you doing here?" Nix asked.

"He came to my rescue," Briar answered, locking the

door behind them. "Don't ask why. He doesn't seem inclined to share his secrets."

She made him sound like a foot-stomping adolescent, Dalton thought. Hell, maybe that's what he'd been acting like for the past few months. He'd be the first to admit he hadn't taken well the earthshaking change in his life history.

"I saw what transpired," Dalton said. "I'll tell you what I remember, though I'm afraid it was too dark for me to have seen anything I could testify to in a court of law."

Nix looked him up and down once, then nodded toward the sofa. "Well, we'll start with what you can tell us and worry about prosecution later. How about that?"

As Dalton followed the detective to the sofa, he spared one last look at Briar Blackwood standing by the door, her arms crossed defensively over her breasts, her thundercloud gaze following him relentlessly across the room.

"WHAT DO YOU think he wants with you?" Dana's voice was little more than a whisper as she walked with Briar into the kitchen.

"He thinks Johnny was part of Cortland's crew," Briar answered just as quietly, moving past the now-sticky kitchen table to grab a clean dishcloth. She drenched the cloth with water from the tap and headed for the table to clean up the mess, starting with Logan's hands and face.

He was grinning now, a strawberry-stained show of little-boy joy that made her heart swell with love. If he was traumatized by what had nearly happened outside only a short while ago, the ice cream had sent it into remission for the time being.

But she couldn't forget as easily. The men who'd accosted her outside her Jeep had tried to pull Logan away from her. In fact, the more she went over events in her mind, the more convinced she was that this attack, at least, had been all about taking Logan.

But why? She wasn't in the middle of a custody battle. Johnny's family saw Logan as much as they cared to, which wasn't that often, and none of them had shown any sign of wanting to change the custody situation. She certainly had no money or possessions to offer as ransom, and anyone who could sneak through the woods quietly enough that she hadn't heard them coming would surely know that much about her financial situation.

Yet she couldn't change the facts of what had happened outside tonight. She couldn't forget the way one of the men had tugged so ferociously at Logan that she'd been terrified, for a heart-stopping moment before the shots rang out, that she would lose her grip on her son and he'd be spirited away, lost from her forever.

"Do you think Johnny could have been working for Cortland?" Dana asked.

Briar had been pondering that question ever since Dalton had raised it at the hospital. Was it possible? She knew Johnny's truck route included Travisville, Virginia, where Cortland Lumber had been located before an explosion destroyed the place not long after Johnny's murder. It was obviously how Johnny had met the woman Dalton Hale believed Johnny had been sleeping with.

But could the man she'd married, the man she'd loved since she was fifteen years old, have gotten involved in the kind of violence and murder Wayne Cortland and his crew of drug dealers, gunrunners and anarchists had spread through the hills for the past couple of years?

The last few years of their marriage had left Briar with few illusions about her childhood sweetheart. He was a better liar than she'd ever credited him to be, and, sadly, she suspected Dalton was probably right about the affair. There'd been other infidelities, as well.

But crossing the line into extortion and murder? Could she really picture Johnny doing such a thing?

She didn't want to believe it. But something had driven a couple of ruthless intruders to her home for two nights in a row.

"I don't know," she answered finally. "But I mean to find out."

"So, WHY ARE you here, anyway?"

Dalton turned his gaze from the head-to-head huddle between Briar Blackwood and Walker Nix, meeting Dana Massey's wary gaze. He shrugged. "Just passing by."

"Convenient timing," she murmured.

"Do you have something you want to say to me? Spit it out."

Dana's lips pressed to a tight line. "I know you hate me right now."

"*Hate* is far too loaded a word," he said quietly. "I don't hate you. I don't know you well enough to feel anything that strong for you."

"And you don't want to."

He shrugged. "Biology isn't destiny."

"Clearly." She pinned him with a long, cool look and moved away.

With a sigh, Dalton looked back at the two cops locked in low conversation on the sofa. From what little he'd overheard of their discussion, Nix seemed to be asking Briar most of the same questions he'd asked Dalton. He hoped Briar was able to fill in more blanks for the detective than he had.

The noise of Briar's Jeep passing close by had jarred him from a doze, but it had taken him several seconds more to drag himself to full consciousness. Several seconds more to see the hulking shadows slinking into the clearing from the woods nearby, and more seconds still to realize that he was watching an ambush unfold. He'd looked away for several seconds to retrieve the rifle and set himself up to fire a warning shot.

In truth, he'd seen little of what had gone on between Briar and her assailants. The one thing he remembered, the one element of the attack that had stuck in his head after the rest had faded into chaos, was how desperately she'd held on to her little boy when one of the attackers had tried to wrest him away.

Clearly, Logan meant everything to her.

The boy was asleep on the sofa beside Briar, curled up under a crocheted throw. Dana had offered to take him to his bed, but Briar hadn't wanted to let him out of her sight. Dalton wondered how she would handle it the next evening when she had to leave him with someone so she could work her patrol shift.

He could solve that problem for her, he realized, the solution weaving itself into place in his sleep-deprived mind. Staying here at this cabin, in the middle of nowhere, only made her and her son more vulnerable to further attacks. Attempts, he corrected himself silently. Tonight hadn't been an attack so much as an attempt to steal Logan away from her.

The question was, why?

Chapter Five

The front door opened without a knock, and Doyle Massey walked in, his eyes widening as he spotted Dalton. Briar watched warily, prepared to jump in if crisis prevention was needed, but Doyle simply let his gaze slide past his half brother and crossed to where Nix and Briar sat. Dana moved from her standing position by the fireplace to join them.

"What's he doing here?" Doyle asked quietly.

"He witnessed the attack," Briar answered in a tone that didn't invite further questions.

Doyle tipped her chin up with his forefinger to get a good look at the bruises on her throat. "Are you and Logan okay?"

"We're fine."

He gave a little wave of his hand toward her injury. "Anybody look at that?"

"I did. In the mirror," she answered flatly. "Just bruises."

Doyle glanced at Nix, as if seeking a second opinion. Nix gave a shrug. Doyle looked back at Briar, his eyes hooded in thought. Then he looked at Dalton Hale across the room and gestured with his head for Dalton to join them. He moved aside to make room for Dalton to join the circle.

Briar glanced up at the county prosecutor, curious to

see his reaction to Doyle's silent command. His gaze met hers briefly, then turned toward the chief, who had begun to speak.

"It's too dark for a search party to do us any good." Doyle's voice lost its earlier gentleness. This was his police-business voice. "Neither of you recognized the two men. No soft ground to allow for footprints. Briar said both men wore gloves, so looking for prints is pointless."

"Are you saying there's nothing you can do to find those guys?" Dalton looked frustrated. "You don't think for a second they'll stop trying, do you?"

"What do you think they want?" Doyle asked him.

"I wasn't here last night, so I can't be sure about what motivated those particular intruders," he answered, his tone measured. "But tonight what I saw was two men trying to take Mrs. Blackwood's son out of her arms. They came here for the boy."

Briar couldn't stop a soft groan from escaping her sore throat at Dalton's confirmation of her worst fear. She'd known the truth the second the man outside her Jeep tried to pull Logan from her arms.

They had come here tonight to take her son.

"I wish I could say I had enough officers available to post a twenty-four-hour guard here," Doyle told her.

She looked up at him. "I know you can't."

"You can move in with me," Nix said.

"No." Dalton shook his head. "Don't you live in a shack in the woods? You think it'll be any safer than this place?"

"It's not a shack," Nix said defensively, but Briar could see that Dalton's words had hit a nerve.

"Do you have a better idea?" Dana asked.

"I do." Dalton took a deep breath, then spoke in a rush, as if he was afraid he wouldn't make it all the way through. "Mrs. Blackwood and her son should come stay with me."

AFTER THE BRIEFEST of stunned pauses, a chorus of *nos* greeted Dalton's offer. From Nix, from Doyle, even from Dana.

But not, Dalton noted with surprise, from Briar.

She just looked at him thoughtfully, her head slightly cocked, as if by changing her perspective she might be able to discern some hidden aspect of his character that had eluded her to this point.

"Before yesterday at the hospital, I doubt you could have pointed out Briar in a crowd." Nix's tone was barely civil. "And now you want to take her and Logan home with you? What's your game?"

"Nix." Briar put her hand on his arm, stepping between him and Dalton. She looked up at Dalton, that same speculative look in her eyes. "Could the rest of you leave us alone a minute?"

"Briar, this isn't a good idea," Doyle said.

"I'm not going to hurt her." Dalton winced inwardly at the hint of injury in his voice. As if Doyle's distrust actually meant anything to him. Which was ridiculous, of course. He owed these people nothing, and he sure as hell didn't care what either of the Massey siblings thought of him.

"Come on." It was Dana who stepped forward and tugged the other two men with her toward the front door. She led them out onto the front porch, shooting Dalton a considering look before closing the door behind them.

"What are you up to?" Briar asked.

"I'm trying to keep you and your son alive."

"Nix is right. Two days ago you didn't have a clue who I was."

"Not entirely true," he disagreed. "For nearly a month now, I've learned almost everything there is to know about you, on paper, at least."

She looked faintly horrified by his answer. "You've been checking up on me? Do you realize how invasive that is?"

"It's my job. You were a person of interest in a case I'm trying to put together against a multistate criminal enterprise."

Her chin stabbed the air between them. "I have nothing to do with Wayne Cortland or anyone who worked for him."

"Your cousin Blake worked for him."

"And I haven't had anything to do with Blake since we were both kids."

"Which I now know because of the background check," he pointed out in what he thought was a perfectly reasonable tone.

But she looked anything but mollified. "I haven't had the opportunity to return the favor." Acid burned the edges of her voice. "I don't know anything about you but what I've read in the newspapers and heard from some very good folks you've treated like garbage for the past few weeks. And you want me to move my son out of the only home he's ever known and into yours? What's in it for you, Mr. Hale?"

"A chance at salvaging what little there is left of my life," he answered before he could stop the bitter words. He stared at her in consternation for a moment before he turned away, raking his fingers through his hair.

After a long silent moment, he felt her hand close over his arm. "I know you've been kicked in the teeth with this whole mess. And I'm real sorry about that. You didn't deserve to be lied to that way all your life. Your daddy and especially your granddaddy let you down something awful. And I can't hold it against you that you want to punch a hole in the world for the wrong it's done you."

He wanted to shake her hand off, to disconnect himself from the warm, gentle weight of her touch. But God help him, nobody had touched him with such compassion in what felt like forever.

His mother was barely holding herself together. His father couldn't bear to look at him anymore, so ashamed was he of his part in the lies and crimes. His grandfather refused to admit to his guilt, choosing self-preserving silence over justice and truth.

All the trouble his grandfather had gone to in order to keep his mother from learning that the son she'd prayed so long to have had died—what good had it done? The truth always came out. Pete Sutherland had been the man who'd taught Dalton that truth years ago as a child.

Had he really thought he could keep this particular truth buried forever?

Dalton hadn't been in his grandfather's position that day at Maryville Mercy Hospital. He hadn't walked into his daughter's room to find his grandson dead in his crib. Maybe the times, the situation, the emotions had all conspired to push Pete Sutherland into the choice he'd made.

But Dalton just couldn't imagine himself taking another woman's baby in order to protect his daughter from pain, regardless of the circumstances, because at best, it was a stalling tactic.

Old Pete hadn't saved his daughter any pain. He'd just pushed it thirty-seven years into the future, after years of lies and schemes and even crimes that made the truth exponentially uglier than it had been that day on the maternity ward at Maryville Mercy. Dalton couldn't turn to Doyle or Dana, even though they'd both indicated, at the beginning, at least, that they would welcome the chance to know him. They couldn't understand what it was like to look at them and see not family but the source of his pain, the strangers who'd blown into town and blown up his world.

It wasn't fair or right. He knew it wasn't. But he couldn't figure out how to stop thinking of them as the enemy.

"What do you want from me?" Briar asked quietly, turning him toward her until he had no choice but to look at her.

There wasn't pity in her gaze, as he'd feared. She looked at him with a mixture of curiosity and, strangely, a hint of understanding.

"I want to bury the Cortland organization once and for all," he answered after gathering his wits. "I want them gone from these hills for good."

"Because you think it's the only thing that will make folks around here forget your family scandal and pull the lever for you in the voting booth."

He shook her hand from his arm and turned away in anger. Not because she'd insulted him but because she was partially right. It might not be his only motive for wanting to see justice done, but it was a big part of it. Maybe too big a part of it.

"I'm not sayin' I won't help you," she said as the silence filling the space between them threatened to smother him. "I just want to be clear on our motives. You want to be elected County Prosecutor. I want to protect my son, and if you're right about Johnny, I want to make right what he did. And I wouldn't mind solving his murder so my son won't have to wonder about all that in years to come."

"I don't think it will be enough to save my ambitions," he said quietly. "But I want the job anyway."

"You could make more money in private practice," she murmured.

He shot her a baleful look, unable to stop his reaction. "I don't care about the money."

"Everybody cares about the money. I know I do." She

waved her hand around the cabin. "You think I live here because I like a drafty cabin with a sometimes-leaky roof? You think I can my own food and kill my own game because I'm part of some organic whole-food locavore movement?" She shook her head. "I live here because it's paid for. I grow and kill my own food because it's cheaper that way, and it allows me to put money away so Logan can go to college and get the hell out of these mountains if that's what he wants. Money matters."

He rubbed his jaw, wondering how many different ways he could make this woman despise him in one short night. "I have all the money I need. You must know that. I have the luxury of choosing a job because it satisfies something more than my bank account."

"Lucky you." She turned away, crossing to the sofa and sitting next to her sleeping son. She gently circled her palm over his back, lowering her voice. "I don't have that luxury. I have to work so we can eat. And I can't afford to put him in day care. Aunt Jenny won't be able to watch him for a while, so you see, I'm in a really desperate situation at the moment."

He waited, realizing she was on the verge of making a decision. Anything he said at this point would probably hurt his chances of getting what he wanted. And though she might not believe it, one of the things he wanted more than anything in the world was to protect her and her son from going through another night like tonight.

She looked up at him. "I would do anything to protect Logan."

"I know."

"I know you know. That's why you're offering to take us in. You know I'd never even consider it otherwise."

He waited, keeping silent. The moment stretched to the breaking point.

"I'll do it." She looked down at her little boy. "But I have some conditions of my own."

He moved slowly toward her, settling on the end of the scuffed pine coffee table in front of the sofa. "What conditions?"

"You let me pay rent."

"It's not necessary."

"I'm not doing it for you. I'm doing it for me."

Pride, he thought, not without admiration. "I need your cooperation, not your money. It's far more valuable to me."

Her gaze snapped up to meet his. "You'll have my cooperation. Matter of fact, I insist on being part of your investigation."

"You already have a job."

"I have time off, too. And I'll spend what I can of that helping you with your investigation. But I get to see everything in your files."

He wasn't sure that condition was even possible to meet. "It's an open investigation—"

"And I'm a Bitterwood police officer. It's a condition of my agreement. I get to see all the files. I might recognize a clue you wouldn't."

He released a sigh. "Okay. But you have to tell me everything you can remember about your late husband's time with Davenport Trucking."

He could see the idea made her uncomfortable, but she finally gave a swift nod and extended her hand toward him. "Agreed."

He took her outstretched hand, closing his fingers over hers. Her handshake was firm and businesslike, her palm dry and callused. He felt a sudden unexpected surge of anger at the feel of that small tough hand rasping against his. God only knew how hard a life she'd lived, trying to make a future for her son. How many more years of struggling and saving still lay ahead of her. The thought of those sons of bitches out there trying to rip her son away from her for who knew what reason—

He caught himself before his rage reached full throttle. There was a lot about her life he couldn't change. But he could do this one thing. He could make the next few weeks of her life as comfortable and secure as he could.

"Let me tell the others," she suggested, releasing his hand and pushing to her feet. "Watch Logan for me?"

He stared after her as she stepped out to the porch and closed the door behind her, realizing what an honor she'd just bestowed on him by trusting him to watch her child alone, even for a few moments with her so close by.

He looked down at the sleeping boy, carefully flattening his hand against his warm, flannel-clad back. He was so tiny, so breakable, Dalton thought, holding his breath as he felt the child's rib cage expand and contract with his slow, deep respirations. And tonight someone had tried to rip him out of his mother's arms, for reasons they still hadn't quite figured out.

"Nobody's going to take you away from your mama," he whispered, his own breathing falling into rhythm with the boy's. "Not on my watch."

POKE, POKE, POKE.

Briar opened one eye and found herself looking up at her son's bright, wide eyes. He poked her again in the ribs and laughed.

"Hey there, mister." She pushed herself up on her elbows and looked around the borrowed bedroom, so unlike her bedroom at home, and wondered how on earth she'd let Dalton Hale convince her to come here to stay.

"I'm hungwy," Logan informed her, patting her cheeks with his little hands. He bounced, too, foot to foot, the springy mattress too great a temptation for an energetic boy his age.

"I bet you are." She hugged him to her, dipping her nose into the curve of his neck for a nice long smell. "Did you find the potty okay?" The guest room had a bathroom of its own, and somehow in the chaos of the previous night, she'd managed to remember his step stool for the bathroom.

Poor Dalton Hale, she remembered with a little smile as she followed Logan to the bathroom. His eyes had grown so huge watching her gather up the necessities of life with a three-year-old, she'd half expected that he'd rescind his offer of a place to stay.

Her watch read nine in the morning. She wondered if Dalton had left for the office already without waking them. He'd given her the grand tour of the place the night before so she'd know where everything was and how to work the security system. But by the time he'd shown her the guest bedroom where she and Logan would sleep, she'd been riding the last fumes of her adrenaline rush. He'd cut the tour short, told her to get some sleep and escaped to his own room before she'd been able to ask about his plans for the next morning.

Holding Logan's hand, she helped him down the long flight of stairs down to the first floor, trying not to gape like a hillbilly on her first trip to town. It wasn't so much that the house was grand and ostentatious—it wasn't, really. It was large and roomy, yes, but it didn't have priceless paintings on the wall or rare sculptures displayed under glass.

But almost everywhere she looked, she saw things that were nothing but luxuries, things that had no purpose beyond looking pretty or drawing the eye to something else. Things that Dalton Hale had bought, not because he needed them or could make use of them but because they'd caught his eye and pleased his tastes.

That's what I want for Logan, she thought. *I want him to be able to have things he likes just because he likes them. And not worry about whether they're taking money away from the things he needs.*

To her surprise, Dalton was still there, perched on one of the breakfast bar stools in the kitchen reading the Knoxville morning newspaper. He looked up and smiled, the expression softening the stern lines of his face.

"Did you sleep okay?" he asked.

"Better than expected. I thought you'd be off to work by now."

"I took the day off." He folded the paper and set it aside, sliding off the stool to crouch in front of Logan, who was half hiding behind Briar. "What would you like for cereal, little man?"

Logan leaned his head around Briar's leg. "Ice cream."

Dalton grinned and looked up at Briar, who shook her head firmly. "I think we'd better have something a little more nutritious."

"He likes peanut butter with sliced bananas on toast," she suggested, trying to think of something even a bachelor might have in his kitchen.

"I can handle that." Logan rose and crossed to the large pantry by the refrigerator. His kitchen, like the rest of his house, was built for convenience and ease of use, with plenty of cabinets and miles of counter space. The breakfast bar doubled as a butcher block, but despite its large size, it barely seemed to make a dent in the spacious room.

"I know folks who'd kill to have a kitchen like this," she said as he brought a jar of peanut butter, a couple of ripe bananas and a bag of sliced bread to the counter. "And no jury in this part of Tennessee would convict them."

"It's too big for one person," he admitted. "But it comes in handy when I entertain."

"Do you do much of that? Entertaining?"

He put four slices of toast in the oversize toaster on the counter nearby. "More than I want to. The price of politics."

She set Logan on one of the stools and perched on the one beside him. "I'll do some shopping for Logan and me sometime today. So we don't eat you out of house and home."

He paused in the middle of twisting the top off the peanut butter jar. "No. You're here as my guests."

"No, we're not." She lifted her chin. "We're here so you can pick my brain about Johnny. And I'm here because you live in a gated community and you have a real nice alarm system. We're not friends."

He looked at her for a long moment, and for a second she thought she saw something that looked suspiciously like hurt in his green eyes. Then he looked down at the open jar of peanut butter and shrugged. "As you wish." He sounded indifferent, not insulted, and she shook off the guilt that had fluttered for a moment in the center of her chest.

"Speaking of that," she added a moment later, "how soon can you get me those files we talked about last night?"

The toast popped up and he gingerly removed the hot bread from the toaster and set it on a paper towel spread across the counter. "I'll have to go into Barrowville to retrieve them, but I think today would be better spent figuring out the logistics of your stay here."

"I work the five-to-midnight shift at the station," she said, reaching for the bananas sitting next to the jar of peanut butter. While Dalton spread peanut butter on the bread, she peeled the bananas and started slicing them into thin rounds and putting them atop the peanut butter and toast. "My aunt has been watching Logan while I'm at work, but she can't deal with him with her arm broken the way it is."

"I took the liberty of calling Laney this morning to discuss the options." He left the counter and walked over to the refrigerator.

"Yeah?"

He pulled a jug of milk from the refrigerator and looked at the expiration date. Wincing, he put it back into the refrigerator and turned to look at her, his expression apologetic. "Will water be okay?"

"Water's fine," she answered, hiding a smile. "What did Laney have to say?"

"My work keeps me in the office until six most nights. It's a ten-minute commute from Barrowville to here, so I can be home by six-fifteen or six-twenty at the latest. I assume you'd need to leave for work around four-thirty in order to have time to change into your uniform and gear, so we're talking about less than a two-hour window of time we need to cover, correct?"

"I suppose so."

"How well behaved is Logan? In general?"

"He's a three-year-old boy. He's impatient and rowdy, but he's not particularly disobedient. It helps if he likes you."

Dalton set a small cup of water in front of Logan and bent to look him in the eye. "You like me pretty well, don't you, Logan?"

Logan looked up at him as if considering the question. "Ice cream?"

"Cupboard love," Briar murmured.

"What I'm thinking is you could leave a little early and drive him by my office when you're ready to go to work.

Laney and I can take turns watching him until it's time to leave the office."

"I don't know about that—" Briar began.

"I can set up a place for him to play. I'll buy him some coloring books and picture books—is he starting to learn to read?"

She nodded. "He has a few favorite books. I brought them with me."

"I can buy duplicates for the office, then. So he'll have the things that are familiar to him."

"You don't have to do that. I can pack them in his little backpack to take with him. But are you sure you want to do this? I don't want him to interfere with your work."

"I'm sure. It's the only thing that makes any sense. The point of bringing him here is to protect him from the people trying to use him against you. Hiring a babysitter neither of us knows isn't going to work, is it?"

She shook her head quickly. "No."

"Do you trust me with him, Briar?" His green eyes were darkly intense as he met her troubled gaze. "Do you trust that I will protect him for you?"

There was no good reason why she should, she knew. He was little more than a stranger to her, and his motives were anything but unselfish. He was bitter and angry at his life at the moment, and even when he wasn't, he possessed the sort of driving ambition that could make a man grow self-focused and myopic.

But for some reason, she found herself nodding in answer to his question. "I do. I trust you to protect him."

"Then it's settled? At least until we try the system and find it wanting?"

"Yes," she said. "But I have a condition."

His eyes narrowed warily. "Another one?"

"Yes. You need to learn how to shoot a gun the right

way. No more of that aiming at the ground and hoping nothing bad happens." She allowed herself a little smile at his expense. "If you're going to try to look like a good ol' boy to win an election, the least you owe your constituents is to walk the walk as well as you talk the talk."

Chapter Six

"How long have you been shooting?" Dalton asked a couple of hours later as he peered at the rather sad results of his first target-practice round. He'd hoped to acquit himself better, but he wasn't surprised to see how badly he'd failed.

Briar tucked an errant curl behind her ear and cocked her head as she studied the holes in the target. "My uncle Corey gave me my cousin Dan's .22 when I turned eight. Dan was getting a bigger one, and Uncle Corey knew I'd been wanting a gun of my own. Of course, my daddy taught me to use a rifle earlier, I guess when I was six or so."

"That young?"

She shot him a look that made him feel like an idiot. "If you're going to have guns in the house with kids around, you need to teach them young that they're not to be toyed with. I've already introduced Logan to my pistol and my shotgun. He knows not to touch them, even if they're not loaded. When he's a little older, I'll teach him how to shoot."

"My father wasn't much of a gun person." Almost as soon as the words escaped his lips, he felt a hot wave of embarrassment flush through him. He felt Briar's gaze on him but he couldn't quite meet her gaze. "Lucky for Dana Massey, huh?"

Not too long ago, his father had taken a few potshots at Dana when she'd started nosing around in her mother's past. Apparently, his father and grandfather had feared she was getting too close to the truth about Dalton's parentage, and they'd decided to take dire steps to stop her. But it had been his father who'd ended up with a bullet in his shoulder and a future in jail stretching out in front of him. "Dana thinks your father didn't really want his shots to hit her. That's why he missed so badly."

Dalton handed her the borrowed rifle and walked a few steps away. "I think he was just a bad shot."

When she didn't say anything else, he ventured a quick look at her. She was just looking at him, a thoughtful expression on her face.

It struck him, not for the first time over the past couple of days, that Briar Blackwood was a pretty woman. It wasn't the kind of polished beauty he met in his work or even the corn-fed cuteness of small-town beauty queens who rode parade floats or won the local pageant crowns. She wasn't wearing a stitch of makeup, and her hair was a mess, but he found he liked looking at her anyway. She had a natural sort of prettiness that came from good health, good genes and, he was beginning to believe, a good soul.

He had seen earlier at his house that she felt out of place there. She'd tried not to let it show, but her poker face wasn't nearly as good as she'd probably like to believe. She didn't enjoy feeling obligated to him, like some poor mountain girl he'd taken pity on.

He didn't pity her, though. She was, in many ways, a remarkable woman. A strong woman, with discipline, integrity and guts.

Dalton had done his homework on Briar Blackwood before he'd ever approached her, looking into the basics of who she was and what kind of life she'd lived before and after marrying Johnny Blackwood. She had been born a Culpepper, and a person didn't grow up in Bitterwood, Tennessee, without knowing a Culpepper was more likely than not to break the law. How she'd dodged that family tradition he didn't know, but her record was clean, and now she was that most rare of creatures, a Ridge County Culpepper who wore a badge.

She'd married Johnny Blackwood when she turned eighteen and remained his wife until Johnny's death nine years later. She'd worked as an emergency services dispatcher while going to community college part-time to get her criminal justice degree. She'd gone through the Bitterwood Police Academy and graduated with honors back in December.

By all accounts, she was a good-hearted, hardworking woman liked by one and all. He certainly couldn't claim such a thing about himself, not since his life had gone so askew. There were plenty of people who didn't care much for him at all, starting with the Bitterwood chief of police.

Doyle had arrived at the rifle range about fifteen minutes ago. Dalton had spotted the chief about the time Briar finished her brief primer on shooting a rifle. Doyle must have seen Logan with Detective Nix, who had agreed to watch the boy at the police station while Briar gave Dalton shooting lessons. No doubt the prospect of watching Dalton make a fool of himself on the range had been too tempting for the chief to resist.

"Doyle's here," he told Briar.

"I know. I saw him earlier." She switched out the target to a new one. "Come on. Let's give it another try."

She'd showed him how to load the rifle earlier, and fortunately, he was a quick study. Her nod of approval when he had finished reloading felt like lavish praise.

"Remember, you're not pulling the trigger. You're pressing it. You want as little movement in the rifle as possible. Don't close your eyes when it fires. You want to keep looking at the target. Guide it in."

He slanted a look at her, and she grinned a little sheepishly.

"I know it sounds like hokum, but the thing is, if you're focusing on getting that round into the target, your whole body is aligned toward that goal and you're just going to make a better shot."

He settled the rifle barrel on the bench rest and sighted the target through the scope.

"And breathe," she added. "Just breathe."

He focused on the target and tried to rid his mind of everything but that one center spot he wanted to hit. But clearing his mind seemed to be something he could no longer do at will.

So he did the next best thing. He focused his thoughts on Briar and Logan. He'd promised to help her protect her son, and if he had to spend hours every day on this range, shooting this bloody rifle and suffering the scrutiny of Doyle Massey, he'd do it. He'd given himself this task, inserted himself into their world for his own purposes.

Competence was the least he owed them.

He pressed the trigger. The rifle kicked but he held it as steady as he could, keeping his eye on the target.

The bullet didn't hit center, but it was close.

"Nice," Briar said softly from her position a few feet away.

He couldn't hold back a satisfied grin.

He took his time and fired the next three rounds into the target. None of the three got as close as the first round, but his aim was considerably improved over his earlier effort.

"Not bad at all," Briar told him as they studied the target more closely. "You're pulling a little to the right with your shots, though. You'll need to figure out how to compensate for that."

Dalton started to answer when he saw Doyle walking toward them behind Briar's back. He tried not to react, but he couldn't seem to keep his lips from pressing into a thin line of annoyance.

"How long are you going to keep hating him for being your mother's son?" Briar asked softly without turning around.

"I don't hate him."

Her eyebrow twitched upward a notch, but she didn't comment.

"Second try was pretty respectable," Doyle commented when he got close. "Pulling a little to the right, but not bad at all."

Dalton wanted to snap out some brilliant cutting remark, but he didn't want to do it in front of Briar. He settled for something milder if not entirely friendly. "Town not keeping you busy, chief?"

"Overseeing the shooting range is part of my job description." Doyle turned his gaze to Briar. "Logan's got my entire station wrapped around his little finger. I'm pretty sure we're about to make him an honorary police officer."

She flashed the chief a toothy grin that made Dalton's breath catch. Damn, but when she smiled, she just lit up everything around her. It made him want to make her smile more often. God knew, she'd had little enough to smile about in her life.

"I'll go take him off Nix's hands," she said, glancing at Dalton. "Chief, would you sign Mr. Hale out of the range for me?"

Dalton opened his mouth to protest, but she was already well down the firing range. He clamped his mouth shut and looked at Doyle.

"How's she doing?" Doyle asked, ignoring the glare Dalton couldn't keep in check.

He sighed. "She's remarkably resilient."

Doyle smiled a little at the description. "She is that." He gestured with his head for Dalton to follow him.

They walked down to the range master's kiosk, where Dalton handed over his visitor's badge and signed out of the range. From there Doyle kept stride with him as they crossed the grassy no-man's-land between the police station and the firing range.

"You've lived here all your life," Doyle said after a few moments of silence. "Has there always been this much trouble with the bad elements around these parts? Or is this something new?"

Dalton was surprised by the question. Not so much by the content as the fact that Doyle spoke as if he actually wanted Dalton's opinion. "It's both, I guess. They were always around—the drug dealers, the militias, even the anarchists. But recently, thanks to Wayne Cortland, they've coalesced. And they're a hell of a lot meaner and more effective now that they've joined forces."

"It's an odd coalition," Doyle mused. "Although I guess maybe it's the anarchy element that's holding them together."

"That and the money. They get to wreak havoc on civilization and make obscene amounts of cash doing it."

"But what do they do with that cash? The elements we're after are still out there in the hills, living like they always did."

Dalton thought about the question for a moment, realizing it was an angle to his investigation he hadn't really given proper thought before. "I don't know. I guess that's something we should find the answer to."

Doyle nodded. "I guess it is."

Dalton stopped as they reached the back entrance of the police station. "I'm investigating what's left of the Cortland crime organization."

Doyle nodded. "I know. I'm engaged to your colleague, remember."

Dalton managed a smile. "I hope you realize how lucky you are to be marrying her."

"I do."

"I don't hate you." Dalton bit his bottom lip as the words spilled from his mouth and hung in the warm air between them. He hadn't meant to blurt them aloud, but he found he wasn't that sorry he had.

Doyle's eyes narrowed slightly, but his lips curved at the corners. "Duly noted."

"I'm not ready to be part of your family, either."

"Nobody expects you to."

He looked away from Doyle's understanding gaze, not willing to go past this declaration of a truce.

"Have you talked to your father recently?" Doyle asked.

The muscles of Dalton's neck and shoulders tightened until they ached. "That's none of your business."

"You're right." Doyle nodded toward the door. "After you."

They walked in silence to the stairs. Once there, Doyle paused, his jaw tightening as he looked up the flight of stairs.

His leg, Dalton thought. The chief had broken his leg a little over a month ago in a car crash.

A car crash Dalton's grandfather had engineered.

Doyle hadn't been out of the cast long. "Take the elevator," Dalton suggested.

Doyle glanced at him. "I need the exercise." He started up the stairs, clearly favoring the bad leg.

"You're a stubborn fool," Dalton called up after him.

Doyle turned at the landing, grinning at him. "Takes one to know one."

Dalton took the steps two at a time, blasting past Doyle before they reached the top.

"Show-off," Doyle muttered.

To Dalton's surprise, he felt a grin creeping over his face in response.

He didn't wait for Doyle, striding quickly down the corridor to the detectives' office, where he found Briar sitting on the edge of Walker Nix's desk, her jean-clad legs dangling as she watched Nix reading one of Logan's books to him while the little boy blinked to stop himself from nodding off. Dalton paused in the doorway, suddenly feeling like an interloper.

Doyle limped up behind him, stopping beside him in the doorway. He looked at the homey little scene for a moment before murmuring, "Nix is like family to Briar."

She thinks the world of him, Dalton thought, watching the smile play across her face. What would he have to do to make her smile at him that way?

And why did it matter?

"What do you really want from them?" Doyle asked softly. His tone wasn't accusatory, Dalton realized. Just curious.

"I want to keep them safe."

"Why?"

Dalton closed his eyes. "I don't know."

Doyle gave him a light thump on his chest as he hobbled past him. "Maybe you should give that some thought."

Briar looked up at the chief's approach, her gaze sliding past Doyle to lock with Dalton's. He felt a shimmery sensation in the center of his chest as those solemn gray eyes held his and a faint smile played across her full lips.

Why did he want so badly to keep them safe, badly

enough to upend his orderly life to bring them into the heart of it?

Doyle was right, as much as Dalton loathed to admit it. He needed to figure out his motives, and quickly. Because he'd worked too hard for too many years to let his plans be derailed by another reckless decision.

DALTON HALE'S GAZE was so focused and relentless that Briar imagined she could feel it brushing across her cheek like a gust of wind. He'd come in with his half brother—had something happened between them on the walk to the station from the firing range? Neither looked any worse for the trip, so she assumed they'd avoided getting into a tangle. But Dalton's silent scrutiny was really starting to wear on her nerves.

"What?" she asked finally after she'd strapped her sleeping son in his car seat in the back of the Jeep.

"What what?" he countered drily.

She opened her own door. "You've been lookin' at me for an hour. Do I have spinach in my teeth?"

"Did you eat spinach today?"

"Don't be so literal." She slid behind the steering wheel.

Dalton's mouth curved as he settled in the passenger seat beside her. "You don't have spinach in your teeth."

"Then what?"

"I heard the chief offer you the night off. Why didn't you take it?"

It wasn't an answer to her question; Dalton's sudden scrutiny had started a while before Doyle had made the offer. But she supposed a question was better than another few minutes of unadulterated appraisal. "I believe in carrying my weight. I don't want special treatment."

"I don't think the chief or anyone else would think otherwise."

"Why don't you call him Doyle?" she asked, even though she knew the question was none of her business. Still, if he could unnerve her by staring at her all afternoon, she supposed she could dig under his skin a bit with an impertinent question. "I know you don't see him as your brother, but he has a name besides *the chief.*"

Dalton's mouth tightened. "I don't know. I suppose it's a way not to think of him as a person."

"That's a lovely sentiment," she drawled.

"You don't know what it's like to learn your whole life is a lie. So you don't have standing to judge how I handle it."

She felt the sting of his quiet rebuke. "I'm sorry. You're right. I don't." She pulled the Jeep out of the police department parking lot.

After a long silence, Dalton spoke, his tone softening. "No, I'm sorry. I know you and everybody else want things to be easier for all of us. I just don't think easy is in the cards."

"My mama always said that nothing worth doin' is easy." She shot him a grin, surprised when he returned it.

"Everybody's mama says that."

"Doesn't mean it's not true." She looked away from that toothy, surprising grin, pressing her hand to her chest as if she could calm the sudden acceleration of her pulse.

"I don't know why I'm doing this," he said a few minutes later, after a steady silence had fallen between them.

She looked away from the road briefly, tightening her grip on the steering wheel. "Letting Logan and me stay at your place?"

"I could have put you in a safe house if I wanted to. I have access to those, you know."

She hadn't realized. "Do you want us to go to one? It's okay if you do. It would probably be better."

"You'd rather go to a safe house?"

Her mind rebelled at the notion of taking her son to some strange place, surrounded by people they didn't know. But wasn't that what she'd done anyway? Dalton Hale was little more than a stranger to them. And his house was like no place she or Logan had ever lived before.

But she felt safe there, she realized. She had no particular reason to feel that way, but she did regardless.

"No," she said, not intending to say so aloud but not really regretting it when she heard the word slip over her tongue.

She felt his gaze on her again, a caress of scrutiny that sent a little shiver of awareness darting down her spine. He released a soft breath, as if he'd been holding it.

"I don't regret asking you to stay with me."

"I don't regret staying." She slanted a quick look toward him. "We'll have to take pains to keep it that way, won't we?"

His only answer was a steady, thoughtful stare.

She turned her attention back to the road, blowing out a tense little breath of her own.

SHE LEFT LOGAN with Dalton around four, explaining that she had an errand to run before she reported for her evening shift at the police station. What she didn't tell him, because she knew he'd object, was that her errand involved returning to her cabin to have a look around.

Nix, who'd driven past her place that morning before he went to the station, had assured her the place had looked untouched. But she couldn't believe intruders who'd invaded her home two nights in a row would give up simply because she'd packed up her son and escaped to a well-secured house in a gated community.

Whatever they'd been looking for, they clearly believed it was located at her house. The attempted kidnapping of her son, she'd come to believe, was to give them leverage against her in case she found what they were hunting before they did.

But what were they looking for? And how could it be so important that they'd rip a child from his mother in order to get their hands on it?

The cabin looked undisturbed as she pulled the Jeep into the gravel drive. She parked and stepped from behind the steering wheel, listening carefully for any unexpected sounds.

A light breeze flowed through the trees, rustling the new leaves and rattling the desiccated limbs of the dead Fraser firs dotting the mountainside. Sunset was still a couple of hours away, but here at the foot of Smoky Ridge, shadows had already begun to creep across the landscape, creating an early, false twilight. Though the temperature was mild even in the shade, Briar tugged the collar of her lightweight jacket closer to her neck and wrestled back a shiver.

You're armed and you're resourceful, she reminded herself as she started a slow circuit of the cabin, her watchful gaze taking in each window, looking for anything out of place.

As she neared the back corner of the cabin, she heard a soft keening noise that stood out from the whisper of the wind through the trees. The low animalistic tone set the hairs on her neck prickling with alarm.

Reaching behind her, she tugged the Glock from its holster and edged toward the corner. She took a fast peek and sucked in a silent breath.

Tommy Barnett, her neighbor down the hollow, lay in her backyard in a sticky pool of his own blood, his pale face staring up at the cloudless sky.

She scanned the area quickly, looking for any sign of

movement that might indicate someone had set a trap for her. She saw nothing but the flutter of leaves in the wind.

Tightening her grip on the Glock, she hurried to Tommy's side, taking a quick assessing look at his injuries. Blood had drenched his blue plaid shirt in the front, pouring from five puncture wounds in his chest and abdomen. By the sheer volume of blood seeping out beneath him, she suspected there might be other wounds she couldn't see.

She pulled out her cell phone and called 911, reporting the situation with the terse, detailed skill of someone who'd once made her living on the other end of the line. "I have to try to stop the bleeding," she told Karen Allen, the dispatcher. "I'm going to have to hang up."

"EMT and police are on the way," Karen assured her.

Briar shoved the phone back into her pocket and assessed the wounds more closely, her heart sinking as she took in the full measure of damage done to her neighbor. There was little she could do at this point, but she tried direct pressure on the wounds in hopes that she could stanch the bleeding long enough for the EMTs to arrive and take over. "Tommy? It's Briar. Can you hear me?"

Tommy's face had turned to a ghastly gray that Briar could barely make herself look at, since she knew what it meant. Death was coming, sure and swift, and she feared there was nothing she could do to stop it.

"Tommy, please hang on. The ambulance is on the way."

His lips moved faintly, a soft gurgling noise spilling from his bloodstained lips. She leaned closer, trying to make out words in the rattle of sound escaping his throat.

"He won't stop," Tommy rasped.

"Who won't stop?" she asked, pressing her fingers to his throat, seeking a pulse that was already growing too weak to discern.

"Blake," he said. "Blake won't stop."

She closed her eyes, not surprised to hear her cousin's name on a dying man's lips. But pained nevertheless, as if she carried the poison of his crimes in her own blood. "Did Blake do this to you?"

Tommy's hand, sticky with blood, closed over her wrist, his grip surprisingly strong. "You can't run far enough."

His grip loosened. His fingers slid away, leaving a streak of blood across her skin. She heard the guttural growl of death laying claim to his prey, then still, hollow silence, as if the man's departing soul had taken with it all the music of life.

She sat back on her heels, tears burning her eyes. A prickling sensation raced through her body, raising the hairs on her arms and legs and setting off tremors low in her belly. She rose slowly to her feet and turned a slow circle, her breath quick and shallow as the woods closed in around her like a tomb.

You can't run far enough.

She was beginning to fear those words were true.

Chapter Seven

"You should have called." Dalton's heart was still racing from the surprise of finding a pale, bloodstained Briar Blackwood standing at his door when he opened it shortly after dinner. She'd calmed his initial fear by assuring him the blood wasn't her own, but the story she'd relayed as he'd helped her out of her jacket had done little to steady his rattling nerves.

"I'm sorry. I didn't want to worry you, and then the chief ordered me home."

He felt a rippling sensation shoot through his chest at her use of the word *home* to describe his house. She seemed to realize her mistake, flashing him a brief humorless smile. "Here, I mean."

"Go get cleaned up," he said gently. "Do you want a drink?" He didn't have much in the house; he hadn't entertained in weeks, thanks to the turmoil in his family, and he wasn't much of a drinker himself. But he could probably find some brandy or something stronger if she needed it.

"Do you have any hot chocolate?" she asked.

He smiled. "Going for the strong stuff, are you?"

She smiled then, a genuine one, not that bleak flash of teeth she'd sent his way earlier. "I like to live on the edge."

He couldn't smile back, realizing how close she'd come to walking into an ambush that evening. Her cousin and his minions couldn't have been gone long if Tommy Barnett had still been alive when she'd found him. From her description of his wounds, the blood loss would have been massive and death quick. "Use my bathroom. Logan's asleep in your room. I don't think he should see you like that."

Her smile faded. "No, you're right. Thank you for thinking of him."

He watched her climb the stairs to her room, feeling the weight of her grief in each weary step she took. When she'd disappeared from view, he turned to the phone to call his office. But it rang before he reached it.

"Dalton Hale," he answered.

"It's Doyle."

The sound of the chief's voice in his ear was, unexpectedly, a relief. "She's here. She's safe."

"I know. I had Nix follow her there."

Of course, Dalton thought. The Bitterwood P.D. took care of their own. Depending on the circumstances, it could be a very good thing. Or a very bad one. He'd seen both situations during his tenure at the Ridge County prosecutor's office. "She's upstairs cleaning up. Do you want to leave a message for her?"

"No, I just wanted to make sure you knew what was going on."

"She told me."

"Did she tell you what Tommy told her before he died?"

"She mentioned he'd implicated her cousin Blake."

"He told her Blake wouldn't stop until he got what he wanted. That she couldn't run far enough."

Dalton felt a flutter of unease run through him. "You think they'll come after her here?"

"I think it's possible. Maybe even likely. Maybe we

should rethink the situation. Put her and Logan under guard."

"I already told her I could put her and Logan in a safe house."

"Really?" Doyle sounded surprised.

"I want her safe."

"Yes, I believe we've established that." Doyle's tone was dry as dust.

"She said she doesn't want to go to a safe house. I haven't asked her tonight, though."

"We mentioned it to her earlier. Maybe you should back out of this setup, Hale."

"Give her no other option?" He recoiled at the idea of abandoning her. "I don't think I can do that."

"Yeah, I didn't really figure you could." Doyle's sigh sounded like a roar through the phone. "I don't suppose you have the funds to hire security?"

"I have the funds," he said.

"Then I'd suggest you contact Sutton Calhoun at The Gates, that new detective agency over in Purgatory. He's married to one of my detectives. He'll set something up for you."

"I know Calhoun," Dalton said quietly. He'd heard of The Gates, as well. They were starting to make waves in the area, mostly for the good. However, some of the people the detective agency was hiring seemed, to Dalton, at least, to be questionable risks. Calhoun was one. The son of Ridge County's most infamous grifter, Calhoun had only recently returned to Bitterwood after years away. He seemed decent enough, Dalton supposed, though it was hard to imagine how Cleve Calhoun's son could be so very far removed from his incorrigible father's criminal ways.

And he'd also heard the agency had recently hired Seth Hammond, Cleve Calhoun's longtime apprentice at the confidence game. Admittedly, the man seemed to have cleaned up his act, even marrying Rachel Davenport, a woman from a well-respected Bitterwood family. But risk was risk, and The Gates seemed a bit reckless about taking more than its share.

"I'll give you his number," Doyle added as the silence between them stretched across the phone line.

"I have it," Dalton answered. "I'll talk to Briar and see what she says."

"Tell her to call if she needs anything."

"Will do." He hung up the phone, leaving his hand on the receiver as he considered whether there was any point in calling his office at this late hour. Some of the other lawyers worked late, but it was nearly eight o'clock now. It wasn't likely that anyone was still around.

And what could anyone do at this point? There was no suspect in custody, and Blake Culpepper was already on the BOLO list; every lawman in the state of Tennessee was already on the lookout for the man.

He dropped his hand away from the phone and went into the kitchen to start making the hot chocolate.

From the floor above, he heard the muted sounds of the shower running, and the image of Briar's body, naked and slick from the soap and water, filled his head so thoroughly he nearly dropped the cocoa mix. He set the can on the counter, his heart pounding like a timpani.

What the hell was he doing? She had just escaped death by moments, had fought and failed to save a friend from death and was even now upstairs washing the man's blood from her skin, and he was thinking of naked breasts and the soap-slick curve of her hips and thighs?

Get a grip, Hale.

He concentrated on the hot chocolate, bypassing the ease of the microwave for the old-fashioned but longer task of boiling water on the stove. By the time he stirred steaming water into two mugs of cocoa mix, the sound of the shower had subsided. In fact, everything upstairs seemed silent and still. He waited several minutes for her to return from upstairs, but she remained wherever she was.

Crossing to the stairs, he gazed upward and listened for sounds of movement from the second floor. But all he heard was the soft hum of electricity coursing through the walls. He had a sudden throat-gripping notion that Blake Culpepper had crept through a window upstairs and spirited Briar and her son away while Dalton remained downstairs, oblivious to the danger.

Before he realized he meant to do it, he had ascended the stairs two at a time and burst into the second-floor hallway.

He strode to the guest room, not bothering to knock on the door before throwing it open to look inside, his pulse throbbing in his ears. Logan lay asleep in the bed, his face cherubic in slumber. Relief swamping him, Dalton crossed to the bed and crouched beside the sleeping child. He touched the little boy's soft hair, pulling back as Logan snuffled softly in his sleep.

As he rose to go, he stopped short at the sight of Briar standing in the open doorway, watching him.

Her eyes were the murky gray of a storm-tossed ocean, hinting at endless depths beneath the reflective surface. Her damp curls framed her scrubbed-clean face, dark against fair. Water drips had left darkened streaks on the heather-gray tank top skimming her curves, including a blotch on her left breast that seemed to cling to the small peak of her nipple, a blatant if inadvertent announcement that she wore no bra beneath the thin cotton.

Below the hem of the tank top peeked a pair of black running shorts that bared the toned perfection of her thighs, the rounded muscles of her calves, a pair of shapely ankles and small slender feet. Her neat toenails, he saw, were painted a bright neon blue.

Heat like a furnace blasted through him and settled, languid and heavy, in his groin. "I thought—" He stopped short, unsure what he'd meant to say.

She stepped back, her head giving a little backward nod, a silent invitation to join her outside. He closed the door behind him, his heart still racing in his chest like a rabbit chased by a fox.

She gazed at him, her lips slightly parted, her breath coming in soft, rapid respirations. In a little blue vein in her temple, her pulse throbbed visibly. Rapidly.

He didn't know how to breathe anymore. His lungs burned for air, but he couldn't draw in enough oxygen to fill them.

Her fathomless gaze drew him closer. He lifted one hand to her face, his fingers brushing aside a tangle of curls to bare the curve of her cheek to his gaze. "I couldn't hear any sounds from up here, and for a minute I thought—"

Her eyes fluttered closed as his fingers skimmed the edge of her jaw.

She was, in so many ways, a hard woman. Tough as the hills that had shaped her from infancy, hard as the rocky soil she tilled to grow the food that fed her and her son. But her skin was silky soft, as if spun from the gossamer mists that shrouded the mountains at sunrise.

The crisp scent of his own shower gel heated by her clean skin filled his lungs, transformed into a heady feminine essence.

Curling his hands into fists, he forced himself to step back from her. One step, then another, until his back flattened against the opposite wall. "I was worried."

Slowly, she slid down the wall and ended up sitting on

the hallway floor, her knees tucked up to her chest. He lowered himself to the floor across from her, grimacing a little as his knees creaked, reminding him he wasn't getting any younger.

"I didn't find Johnny's body when he died." Her gaze settled somewhere around the middle of his chest. "But I made them let me see him afterward. In the morgue."

He knew. He'd read the case file already. More than once. He'd read transcripts of interviews, the autopsy report, the detective's report, the coroner's inquest. "Did tonight bring it back?"

She rubbed her chin with her thumb, her gaze slowly lifting to his. "I won't be surprised if they prove the same knife that killed Johnny killed Tommy, as well."

He wouldn't be, either.

"Why did they kill Tommy, though? Did he surprise them in the middle of something?"

"What do you think?" he asked.

She shook her head. "I don't know. I think maybe I'm afraid to know."

A thought occurred to him suddenly. "You don't blame yourself for this, do you?"

She looked down at her feet.

"Don't. You're not to blame here."

She looked up slowly. "They want something they think I have. But I don't know what it is. Or why it's worth killing for."

Dalton wasn't sure, either. "It would have to be big. Dangerous to more than just one person."

"Why dangerous to more than just one person?"

"You've already told us that you don't think the two men who tried to take Logan were the same men who broke into your house the night before, right?"

She nodded thoughtfully.

"And none of them was your cousin Blake."

"Definitely not."

"But tonight your neighbor mentioned Blake by name, right?"

"Yes." She looked down at her feet again, as if studying those brightly painted toenails. "So either Blake was there or he sent more people in his stead. Maybe the same people as before. Maybe not."

Dalton watched the play of emotions across her downcast face. "That's at least five people involved, right? The four we know about for sure plus Blake. Maybe more."

"That's a lot of people."

"They're protecting something corporate. Not private."

"But what?" She looked up at him suddenly, her gaze so intense it sent a little rattle skittering down his spine.

"Something they fear enough to take big chances," he answered after a moment of thought. "Something that's worth walking into the home of a cop and taking a look around."

"Something worth trying to steal a child from the arms of that same cop. A cop they knew would be armed." Her eyes narrowed. "Something they think I have or know how to get."

"Any ideas?" he asked.

"Only theories," she answered.

"Care to share?"

She moved suddenly, sliding back up the wall almost as quickly as she'd sat. He levered himself to his feet with much less grace, the twinges in his limbs an unmistakable reminder that he was on the downhill slide to forty these days. Almost a decade older than his nimble hallway companion.

With a slight nod of her head the only invitation to follow, she started down the stairs to the first floor.

He followed her into the kitchen, watching as she picked up one of the cups of hot chocolate, took a sip and grimaced.

"Cold," she said. She put both mugs in the microwave, set the timer and turned to face him, leaning back against the counter. Her eyes followed his movements with an almost feral wariness, and he wondered if she was remembering their electric encounter in the hallway.

To ease her tension—and his own—he took a seat at the breakfast bar, putting a layer of granite countertop and polished oak between them. "You have theories?" he prompted.

"I've been thinking about what you've told me about your investigation. How you think Johnny fit in. And I keep going back to the Davenport Trucking connection. Has anyone ever established how a lumber-yard owner in Travisville, Virginia, even got interested in a Tennessee trucking company in the first place?"

"We're pretty sure what caught Wayne Cortland's attention was the fact that Davenport had contracts with the Oak Ridge National Laboratory," Dalton said. "It's guesswork at this point, now that Cortland's dead, but we think he was planning to cause a scare at the nuclear research facility in hopes that it would stop or at least delay oil-shale exploration and production in the area."

He could tell by the look on her face that this information was new to her. "He wanted to stop oil-shale production? Why?"

"He controlled a lot of people in a lot of areas that can be charitably called wilderness. He liked it that way—fewer eyes mean fewer chances to be caught doing something illegal. His network thrived on isolation and people who live on the fringes of society and like it that way."

"And oil-shale production means less wilderness and more people."

He nodded. "More eyes. Exactly."

"He wanted to use a Davenport truck to deliver something to Oak Ridge that would pose a threat, then. Something that might cause a nuclear incident."

"We don't think he was planning to do anything horribly damaging." The microwave dinged and Dalton retrieved the two cups of hot chocolate. He gave her the cup she'd sipped from, keeping the other for himself. "Careful. It's pretty hot."

She looked up at him, her expression curious. "Do you think they were planning to use Johnny to drive the truck that would get into Oak Ridge and cause the trouble?"

"I'm not sure. I just know Johnny seemed to be asking a lot of questions at Cortland. Questions that even that pretty little bookkeeper noticed. If she noticed, other people might have, as well."

"You think that's why he was killed."

"I think it's possible."

She sipped her hot chocolate, her expression hard to read.

"Were you and Johnny happy?" he asked, regretting the words the second they spilled from his lips.

She looked up sharply. "Does it matter?"

He shook his head.

She set the cup of hot chocolate on the breakfast bar counter. "I told you, the same day he died, I started divorce proceedings."

"I know."

She cupped her hands around the mug. "I did love him. He was my first everything. You know? But he never grew up. The woman in Virginia—I know she wasn't the first one. And I couldn't keep myself and Logan in that kind of situation. So I started looking into my options."

"And then he was murdered."

She looked up at him. "I was lucky I had an alibi, huh?"

The urge to reach out and smooth those little frown lines from her face was so overwhelming he had to curl his hands around his hot-chocolate mug to control it. "Why don't you try to catch up on a little sleep, since you have the night off?"

She shook her head, turning to pour out the remains of her hot chocolate into the sink. "I'm okay now. There's no reason why I can't go back to the station and put in some hours."

"I thought they ordered you home."

She shrugged. "I'm ordering myself back." She started toward the stairs, then suddenly stopped, turning to look at him. "If Logan wakes up, he may want you to read him a story. Is that okay? His books are in a bag in the guest room closet."

Dalton smiled. "I can do that."

The faint smile she offered in return made his chest ache a little. She turned and continued upstairs.

As he was pouring the rest of his own hot chocolate down the drain, his cell phone rang. He dug it from his pocket and checked the display. With a sigh, he answered. "Hi, Mom."

"You didn't call me about lunch today."

He closed his eyes, grimacing. "I'm sorry. Things have gotten real crazy around here all of a sudden. Rain check?"

"How about tomorrow? I can meet you at the Sequoyah House Tea Room around noon."

He could tell from her tone that she wouldn't take no for an answer. "Okay. Sequoyah House tomorrow, noon. How're you doing, Mom? Everything okay?"

"I'm well," she answered sparely. "I'll see you at noon."

He hung up and shoved his phone in his pocket, both wishing he could get out of lunch with his mother and hating himself for feeling that way.

His father and grandfather had hurt a lot of people with their lies and machinations.

Including the people they were supposed to be protecting.

Chapter Eight

The doorbell chime startled Briar from a light doze on the sofa. Curled up on the cushion beside her, Logan was still napping, but that wouldn't last long if whoever was leaning on the doorbell didn't give it a rest.

She put down the book she'd been reading and grabbed the Glock from her waistband holster, standing on tiptoe to reach the security lens set high into the solid oak of Dalton Hale's front door. The fish-eye lens revealed Walker Nix's face, to her relief. She holstered the Glock, twisted open the deadbolt and unlatched the security chain to let him in. "Aren't you on duty?" she asked, keeping her voice low.

"Good morning to you, too," he whispered, stepping inside.

"Logan's asleep." She locked the door and led him into the kitchen.

He sat, looking around. "Nice digs. Never been here before."

She grinned at him. "What, you're not on the Sutherland/Hale society guest list? I thought you Nixes were one of the oldest families in the hills."

"Oh, we are. That might be the problem."

Chuckling, she perched next to him. "What are you doing here?"

"Just checking on you. Seeing how Hale's treating y'all."

"Very kindly, actually," she answered with a smile.

"You sound like you actually like the guy."

She shrugged, thinking about that brief tension-strung moment she and Dalton had shared in the upstairs hall the night before. She'd put it from her mind, filed it away under Things That Don't Need to Be Repeated, but the memory seemed to have a rebellious streak. So she'd found the man more attractive than she'd expected. That didn't mean she needed to act on it.

"He's nice," she said when it became clear that Nix was waiting for something more than a shrug. "Logan seems to really like him, too."

Nix nudged her with his shoulder. "What makes you say that?"

She slanted a look at him. "Jealous? Afraid Logan may end up liking him more than he likes you?"

"He *can* afford better toys."

"Logan adores you. But you're never going to be his daddy." As soon as the words came out of her mouth, she realized how they sounded. "Not that Dalton can— I mean—"

"Don't get any ideas about him, Briar." Nix's smile faded.

"I haven't."

"He'd be damned lucky to have you, of course."

"Of course." She smiled, though beneath the humor was a little sting.

"I just think there's a reason why he's thirty-seven and still single."

She blinked. "You think he's gay?"

Nix shot her a look of amusement. "Should I?"

She thought about that moment in the hall again and shook her head. She hadn't imagined the way his eyes had darkened when he touched her or the tremble in his fingers. "No, I don't think so."

"He was engaged once. A long time ago. Her name was Calinda Morgan." Nix smiled a distant smile. "Prettiest girl at Ridge County High School. Everybody wanted her, but Dalton Hale was the one she wanted. Everybody thought they'd marry. Then his granddaddy sent him to Harvard Law, while Calinda stayed behind. A couple of years later, she met another guy, broke it off with Hale and got married."

"Old Pete sent him to Harvard after college? Right about the time Tallie Cumberland and her husband came to town looking for him...."

"I hadn't thought about it before, but yeah. It would have been right about that time." Nix shook his head. "All I know is, when Calinda ended things with him, Dalton took it pretty hard."

"And he's never been serious with another woman since?"

"Not really. I mean, he dates all the time. He's forever getting his picture in the paper, and there's usually some pretty blonde on his arm."

"Blondes, huh?" She said it lightly, to cover the disconcerting quiver in the pit of her stomach.

Nix tugged one of her dark curls. "Tough luck, Briar Rose. You'll just have to find some other rich bachelor now."

She was relieved when they moved on to the topic of Nix's relationship with Dana Massey. "Things still going well with you two?" she asked.

"Gotta show you something." He reached into his coat pocket and brought out a small, velvet ring box.

"Oh, my God," Briar said, her heart rate jumping as she

realized what it was. "You're going to do it, aren't you? You're gettin' hitched!"

"If she says yes." He flipped open the box to reveal a square-cut diamond set in a simple white-gold band. "It's small, I know—"

"It's beautiful. It's perfect. She's going to love it!" Briar threw her arms around Nix and gave him a tight hug. "Look at you, steppin' up!"

He laughed, the happiness transforming his dark face. She realized with quiet wonder that her old friend had become a brand-new man since he met and fell in love with Dana Massey. *That's how it's supposed to be,* she thought. *That's what love's supposed to do to you.*

After almost a decade of marriage, Johnny had still been the same overgrown teenager she'd married. And had she really changed, either?

Maybe their relationship had been doomed from the start.

"WHEN WAS THE last time you talked to your father?"

It had taken his mother almost twenty minutes of small talk to get around to her real point for meeting him for lunch, Dalton thought, laying his fork on the table by his plate. "I'm not sure. A few weeks."

"Four weeks," she corrected mildly. "He thought you wanted to help him."

"I did."

Nina Hale's eyebrows lifted slightly at his use of the past tense. "I know he hurt you. He hurt me, too. And I can't even think about what my father did without wanting to cry my eyes out."

He reached across the restaurant table and touched his mother's hand. Just a light touch, nothing too maudlin. Not in a public place like the Sequoyah House Tea Room.

Sutherlands and Hales didn't perform for an audience. "I'm sorry, Mom. I'm not a defense attorney. I prosecute lawbreakers. I can't defend them."

"He's your father."

He almost snapped out a denial but stopped short, curling his fist around the napkin in his lap. "I secured a very good attorney out of Knoxville. He's getting the best defense available to him."

"He doesn't need the best defense available. He needs his son."

"Mom—"

"He doesn't deserve to be cut off from you. He did what he did for you."

Dalton shook his head. "He did it for himself. For you. Probably for Pete, as well. But he covered up the murder of two people who did nothing wrong. He tried to shoot my—" He stopped short, shocked by the word still lingering in his mind unspoken. "He tried to shoot a deputy U.S. marshal."

"He didn't get close to hitting her."

Dalton stared at his mother. "You don't fire a gun at a person unless you're willing to risk hitting them. He may have been relieved she wasn't hurt, in the end, but he was willing to take the risk that she might be. Don't defend what he did."

"He didn't want to lose you."

"Mother, I was twenty-one years old when he learned the truth. I was a college graduate, living on my own. How could he lose me at that point?"

"Apparently by making a wrong choice," she murmured, her voice controlled but the expression in her eyes bleak.

Dalton sighed. "He hasn't lost me. I will forgive him. I just need time to deal with the betrayal."

"Betrayal?"

"I trusted him to tell the truth when it was important. And he didn't." A cavern-dark bubble of bleak emotion burned his throat. He'd fought so hard to keep from admitting, in front of Doyle or Dana, at least, that he gave any real credence to the story of his origins. All for show, of course. He'd known the first time he'd laid eyes on Dana Massey that his world was already changing. He'd seen the resemblance. Wondered what it meant.

Ultimately, his father's confession had been a release. An answer to doubts that had played in his head over and over from the first time he looked into a stranger's eyes and saw his own.

"Did you know I had another brother?" he asked aloud. "Three siblings. After growing up an only child. Lucky me."

"I would have given you brothers and sisters if I could," Nina said.

"I know. But I had another brother." One he'd never met and never would.

"I spoke to Doyle Massey," Nina said.

Dalton looked at her. "Why?"

"I ran into him in town. He introduced himself."

"I'll tell him to leave you alone."

"I don't need you to protect me from him. He was polite. And kind." Nina took a long slow sip of tea and replaced the china cup carefully on its saucer before she continued. "I liked him, actually. He smiles a lot."

A tearing sensation rippled through his chest. He buried it deep, though he knew it could stay contained only so long. "Why are you telling me this?"

"I understand you've brought a woman to your house to live with you."

Small-town gossip was more efficient than a CIA operation. "She's a potential witness in a case I'm investigating."

"She's a police officer, they say. Is she pretty?"

"It's business."

"Is she pretty?" Nina repeated, emphasizing each word.

"Yes."

"Does that pose a problem for you? Living in the same house?"

"I don't want to have this conversation."

"No, I don't suppose you do." She took another sip of tea. "It could affect your campaign. Having her there."

Ah. His campaign manager, Matt Merrick, had run an end around and spoken to his mother. "Did Merry give you any other helpful suggestions to pass along?"

To his surprise, his mother's lips curved upward around the rim of her teacup. "No, just the one."

"I'm not sleeping with her," he said, trying to ignore the memory of Briar's long toned legs, perfect round breasts and the smell of his bath gel on her warm skin. "She has a three-year-old son, staying there with us. I couldn't ask for a more efficient chaperone."

"Her husband died a few months ago. Murdered?"

"Mother."

"I hate when you call me Mother. It means I've disappointed you."

He closed his eyes briefly. "You told me gossip is an evil. Remember?"

"Well, apparently it's the only way I get to find out what's going on with my son these days."

"Fine." He pushed away his plate, the food mostly untouched. "I'll go see Dad."

"Is she in danger?" she asked, ignoring his offer.

He released a long breath. "Yes. Her son even more so."

"Are you prepared to protect them? Your last Tae Kwon Do lesson was a while ago."

He laughed. "She's a much better shot than I am. In fact, she took me to the firing range for lessons yesterday."

"You *do* like her," Nina said with a hint of a smile. "Don't you?"

"Mom…."

"She's a Culpepper. I guess by now you've heard a few things about the Culpeppers from these parts."

"Don't be a snob, Mother."

She didn't hide her smile behind her cup that time. "Sweetheart, I'm not the snob of the family. Besides, the Cumberlands had a far worse reputation. Yet I love you beyond distraction."

He stared across the table at her, surprised both by the stark declaration of his true maternal origins and by her placid delivery of that painful fact. "Did you ever meet my— Did you meet Tallie?"

"I met her in the park one day when you were about a year old. I didn't know who she was then, of course. I had no idea what your father and grandfather had done. And we'd never seen her before, you see. She'd been a juvenile when she gave birth to you, so they didn't identify her in the papers or show a photo. But I know it was her. She looked a great deal like your sister, Dana, you know. But younger then. She couldn't have been more than eighteen at the time." Nina's gaze seemed to recede from the present, as if she could see that moment in the past playing out before her eyes. "She was so taken with you. Of course, I was mad about you myself, so it didn't seem strange that another person would have found you just as captivating."

"Dana told me that moment was when Tallie decided to stop trying to convince people I was her son," he said quietly. "She saw how much you loved me. And how much I loved you. *Love,* sweetheart. How much I *love* you. How much you love me."

"Always."

To his surprise, she reached over the table and clasped both his hands, squeezing tightly. "Your police officer friend loves her son just as much?"

He nodded. "Every bit as much."

"Then tell Merry to mind his own business."

He walked her to her car after lunch, giving her a swift impulsive hug as she started to unlock the door. "Thanks for lunch. I needed it."

She smiled up at him. "I don't care what that DNA test says. You're my son. And I'll say that to anyone who asks." Her smile drifted away, her blue eyes growing suddenly serious. "But I would never make you choose between me and your brother and sister. They seem like good people, and they're no more at fault for what happened than you or I."

He kissed the top of her head, breathing in deeply the rosewater scent of her, the light floral essence that could take him back to his earliest childhood memories. "I'll keep that in mind."

The rest of his afternoon seemed to drag, dedicated as it was to catching up on outstanding paperwork before running back through his compiled files on the Wayne Cortland crime organization one more time. He'd promised Briar access to these files, he remembered. He called his secretary, Janet, into his office and asked her to make copies of everything before the end of the day. Janet gave him an odd look but took the files and headed off to do what he'd asked.

Around three-thirty his phone rang. It was Briar. "I thought I'd check to make sure it's okay to bring Logan by before my shift starts."

"I'll be waiting. Be sure to bring plenty of things for him to play with in case I can't get out of here early."

"Will do. See you in a bit." She hung up before he could ask her how her day had been.

He leaned back in his chair and gazed out the large picture window that took up a large portion of his eastern wall. From his third-floor office, he had a stunning view of the Smoky Mountains. Sunlight bathed them in a warm golden glow, though it wouldn't be long until twilight painted them in cool hues of blue and purple.

His grandfather hadn't wanted him to stay in Tennessee after college, he remembered. He'd wanted him to go see the world, or at least, that's what he'd said at the time.

Now Dalton wondered if he'd been determined to keep him away from Tennessee until he figured out what to do about Tallie Cumberland.

The office door opened and Janet looked in. "You have a visitor."

Briar had made good time, he thought. But it wasn't Briar who walked through the door. Instead, a willowy blonde entered, dressed impeccably in a flattering navy skirt and jacket, four-inch heels and a crocodile purse that had probably cost a fortune.

"Lydia." He rose as she strode toward his desk, her hair swinging in shimmery golden waves.

"You didn't return my calls." She walked around to perch on his desk, looking up at him with a mixture of irritation and affection.

She'd called twice that morning while he was catching up on the work he'd missed the day before. He'd sent her calls straight to voice mail, meaning to get back to her after lunch. He'd forgotten all about it. "I'm sorry. I took the day off yesterday and I've had to race to catch up."

"Well, I hope you have, because I managed reservations at Chez Berubi in town. Seven-thirty sharp."

He looked at her in dismay. "Seven-thirty tonight?"

Her smile collapsed. "Yes, tonight. We planned this last week."

He looked at her in consternation. She was right, of course. He'd put her off for a week because his caseload had been busy; this week was supposed to have been free of any court appearances.

But that was before Briar and Logan had crashed into his life.

"Lydia, I can't make it tonight. Something's come up—"

Her eyebrows lifted. "I beg your pardon?"

A quick knock on the door interrupted, and Janet stuck her head through the opening again. "Two visitors this time."

Before he could speak, Briar walked in with Logan on her left hip and a fuzzy turtle-shaped backpack slung over her shoulder. She stopped short at the sight of Lydia perched on his desk. "Sorry. Didn't mean to interrupt."

Lydia took one look at Briar and Logan and turned her chilly blue gaze toward Dalton. "Something came up?"

He looked at Briar, who was watching him through narrowed eyes. She shifted Logan's weight to tuck him more securely against her side. "I can find someone else to watch him," she said, already turning toward the door.

"No," he said quickly, moving around the desk, past Lydia, to stop her.

She paused, looking down at his hand on her arm. "It's okay. You've gone above and beyond already. I can probably catch Nix before he leaves."

"It's not necessary." He smiled at Logan, who was watching him shyly from his mother's shoulder. "Logan and I had plans for tonight, didn't we?"

"You and Logan weren't the only ones," Lydia muttered.

He turned to look at her. "Lydia, I'm sorry. I forgot

about our plans. I didn't realize they were set in stone, and you didn't follow up—"

"I left messages that you never returned." Lydia's voice was as sharp as jagged glass.

He felt like a heel, mostly because it seemed he'd just driven the final nail in yet another relationship—and he wasn't particularly upset by it. "I'm sorry."

"What, not even a request for a rain check?"

He hesitated, acutely aware of Briar's watchful gaze. "Lydia, I'm sorry. I just don't think I'm going to have the time to be a proper escort—"

She actually flinched at his choice of words. "Escort? That certainly clarifies things, doesn't it?" Grabbing her purse, she rose and walked to the door, pausing for a moment to look down at Briar and Logan. "Hope you don't have any expectations where he's concerned," she said. "He's not exactly reliable."

She gave the door a sharp jerk, slamming it closed behind her.

Dalton dropped heavily in his chair. "Sorry about that."

"You should go after her. I really can find someone else to watch Logan tonight—"

"The problem is," he said wearily, "I don't want to go after her."

"Oh."

He rubbed his gritty eyes. "You may have picked the wrong person to keep you and Logan safe. Clearly, my life is falling apart these days."

She sat in the chair across from his desk, waiting silently for him to look at her. When he did, she shot him a brief smile. "First, I didn't pick you for anything. You picked us. And second, I don't know anyone in this world whose life doesn't fall apart now and then. Now's just your turn. So quit kickin' yourself about it." She set Logan down on the floor and gave him the turtle backpack. "Logan, why don't you go over there in the corner and get your trucks out to play with?"

Logan looked up at her warily but took the pack in his arms and toddled off to the corner to start unpacking his toys.

"I left his car seat with your secretary. If you'll go sit down with him and play trucks for a little bit, I'll slip out and he probably won't even notice I'm gone," she said, nodding toward her son. "I need to head out soon."

She looked uncertain, as if she doubted he could keep her son from fretting when she left. He took it as a challenge, levering himself down to a cross-legged position on the floor beside Logan. "Can I play?"

Logan looked up at him soberly for a moment, then picked up a little blue police car and handed it to him. "Mama police."

Dalton glanced at Briar, who had edged toward the door. "That's right. Mama's a police officer." When he looked up again, she was gone.

Logan didn't notice her departure for several minutes, and by the time he did, Dalton had given up all pretense that he'd be able to get any work done for the rest of the day. "Why don't we pack up and head home, Logan?"

"Okeydokey," Logan said with a lopsided grin that made Dalton's heart do strange flip-floppy things in his chest. He helped Dalton pack his toys and reached up one small hand to be held. "Go now?"

Dalton let Logan wrap his hand around his index finger. "Sure thing."

The parking lot was still full of cars, as the county-courthouse workday was still at least an hour away from coming to an end. As Logan's short legs struggled to keep up with Dalton's longer strides, Dalton coaxed the boy onto his hip, looping the car seat and backpack over his free hand.

Logan held himself at arm's length at first, but after a few steps, he melted into Dalton's grasp, pressing his forehead into the curve of Dalton's neck. The flip-floppy sensation in Dalton's chest rushed back with a vengeance, and by the time he reached his car, he was grinning like an idiot.

Briar had explained how the car seat worked earlier that morning before he left for the office, and fortunately, he was pretty good at following directions. The seat fit snugly on the bench seat of the pickup truck, and Logan didn't whine too much about being strapped in once Dalton handed over the backpack full of toys.

The drive from Barrowville went quickly since they were ahead of rush hour. As they neared Edgewood, Dalton made a spur-of-the-moment decision to stop at the convenience store about a block from the subdivision to pick up milk and cereal for Logan's breakfast the next morning.

Logan actually reached for him this time when he went to unbuckle him from the car seat. Dalton gave him a quick hug and lowered him to the ground. "You like cereal, Logan, my man?"

"Cheerios!"

Of course. Dalton held out his hand, and Logan curled his fingers around his index finger again. They entered the convenience store and went straight back to the coolers for a half gallon of milk.

"How are you doing with your reading, Logan? Think you can help me find the Cheerios?"

Logan applied himself to the task, grinning brightly when he located the box in the dry-goods aisle. "Cheerios," he announced.

Logan picked up a box and added it to the basket with the milk. They headed to the front to pay.

The clerk was a weary-faced girl in her twenties with lanky blond hair and makeup slightly smeared by a day's work. But she grinned brightly at Logan. "Ain't you a cutie?"

Dalton paid for the milk and cereal, smiled at the clerk and nudged Logan out the door, trying not to think too hard about how much he was enjoying playing Daddy for a little while.

"You and I are going to have a fun time tonight, Logan, my man."

Logan grinned up at him, making Dalton smile in return.

But his smile faded quickly when a dark-clad figure rose from a crouch beside his truck. He wore a camouflage hat low on his head and his face was masked with smears of sooty camouflage face paint. His hulking appearance out of nowhere was such a shock to Dalton that he froze for a moment, half certain he'd conjured the man from his anxiety-fueled imagination.

Then the sinking sun sparked off the large-bladed hunting knife the man brandished in his right hand, and Dalton knew all the wishing in the world wouldn't drive this vision away.

The man in black spoke with a low mountain twang, full of bridled violence, that sent a shudder down Dalton's spine. "If you want to live, give me the kid and get the hell out of here."

Chapter Nine

Dalton had prosecuted his share of violent-crime cases over the ten years he'd worked for the Ridge County prosecutor's office. He'd comforted witnesses and helped them prepare for testimony. And the one thing they'd told him that had always seemed strange was how tunnel-visioned they became when confronted with violence.

"All you see is the gun in your face," one woman had told him after she and her husband had been robbed at gunpoint. "You don't even let yourself look at the person holding it. You just keep looking at the gun. It's like you think as long as you look at the gun, it won't do anything to you."

He understood now. All he could do was stare at the enormous glittering blade of the hunting knife waving in front of his face, to the point that he almost lost his grip on Logan's tiny hand.

Logan had started crying, his little body wrapping around Dalton's leg as if he were trying to hide there. The sound of his soft cries was like a spur in Dalton's side, prodding him to action.

His rifle was in the truck, locked up. He didn't even have a pocketknife on him, but it would have been no match for the enormous blade in the other man's hand anyway.

But he had a half gallon of milk dangling in a bag clutched in his right hand. Five pounds' worth of bludgeon.

He feinted to the left, drawing the knife and the man behind it in that direction. His other hand he swung in an arc, slamming the jug of milk against the man's hand.

The black-clad man didn't lose hold of the knife, but the blow knocked him sideways into the car parked next to Dalton's truck. Dalton hoped it would be enough. Grabbing up Logan, he started running back toward the convenience store.

Sharp stabbing pain raced through his side, and he almost lost his grip on Logan. He felt a tearing sensation, heard the rip of fabric, but he didn't stop running, even as footsteps pounded after him.

There was another customer coming out of the convenience store as he reached the door, a young man in his mid-twenties with shaggy hair and a patchy beard. His eyes widening, he reached out and grabbed Dalton by the arm, his grip amazingly strong. For a moment Dalton tried to shake him off, until he realized the man was dragging him into the store. As Dalton stumbled forward, the younger man threw the deadbolt on the door, locking them both in.

Dalton regained his balance and turned to look at the storefront windows. Standing in the full-glass doorway, knife raised, the dark-clad man with the face paint glared back at him through the glass, his pale eyes blazing with fury. He pounded the butt of his knife against the door, making the glass rattle.

"Call the police," Dalton gasped, turning his body to shield Logan from the man outside.

"They're on the way," the woman behind the counter told him. He looked up to find that she was holding a shotgun gripped tightly in her hands, her gaze on the door.

"Hey, mister, you're bleeding." The young man who'd

pulled him into the store put his hand on Dalton's arm, setting his nerves jangling again. A faint ringing started in his ears and he grabbed for the cashier's desk as the world started to spin around him.

The man tried to pull Logan from his arms, but Dalton held on tightly, pressing the crying baby against his chest as he slid to the floor.

THE CALL HAD come over the radio around five-fifteen. 10-52—armed robbery—with a 10-39, injured person. Briar and her patrol partner, Thurman Gowdy, were the closest unit and responded within minutes. A fire-and-rescue unit had responded, as well, flashing cherry lights strobing the convenience store parking lot as Gowdy pulled the patrol unit into an open parking space.

They made their watchful way into the convenience store, where the action seemed to be focused. Several people stood in a semicircle around two paramedics crouched in front of the cashier's desk. One of the two men, speaking in a low, soothing voice, said, "It's okay now. You can let him go. We'll take good care of him."

"No," a pain-filled voice gritted out. "He stays with me."

Briar's heart jumped in her chest. That was Dalton Hale's voice.

"Police," she announced, moving past Gowdy and pushing her way through the gathered crowd. Dalton Hale sat slumped on the floor in front of the cashier's counter, his arms curled around her son's body. Logan had been crying, but at the moment he was silent, just blinking with confusion at the people standing in a ring around him.

Dalton looked up at the sound of her voice, his green eyes melting with relief. "He's okay," he said.

Logan spotted her and started wriggling to get loose. Dalton let him go, his arms dropping to his side.

Briar scooped her son into her arms, staring at Dalton. He was bleeding from his right side, she could see now. Not a lot, but enough that blood had begun to pool on the floor beside him.

The paramedics moved in quickly, coaxing him onto his back.

"I didn't let him take Logan," Dalton said, his gaze still locked with hers.

Briar looked at Thurman Gowdy. He stared back, then thumbed the shoulder radio and called for backup.

She carried Logan over to the checkout stand and set him on the glass-top counter, quickly looking him over for any signs of injury. He was still making soft hiccupping sounds, and his nose was running from his earlier tears, but she didn't find any sign of injury. "How you doing, buddy?" she asked, pressing a fervent kiss to the top of his head.

"Dallen?" Logan craned his head for a look at Dalton, who was being poked and prodded by the EMTs trying to assess his condition.

"Dalton's going to be fine." *Please be fine,* she added silently.

Gowdy caught up with her a few minutes later. A thin balding man in his late fifties, Gowdy had been a fixture in Bitterwood P.D.'s patrol unit since he joined the force almost forty years earlier. He'd turned down dozens of promotions over the years, preferring to ride patrol, and now he was the go-to officer when there was a rookie cop in need of a senior partner. "I'm not detective material," he'd told Briar on their first day together on the job. "But if you listen to me, you'll learn a hell of a lot about police work in a short amount of time."

Right now he gave her a quick update on what had happened. "Bearded white male, mid-twenties, wearing a dark shirt, dark pants, camo cap and camo face paint. Carrying a hunting knife. Witnesses say he confronted the vic there on the floor. The vic swung his groceries at the guy, grabbed up the little fella here and ran for the store. Someone inside let him in and locked the door before the perp with the knife could get in." Thurman put his hand on her shoulder. "This is your baby, ain't it?"

Briar stroked Logan's mussed hair off his damp forehead. "Yes. The vic is Dalton Hale."

Thurman's eyebrows lifted. "The prosecutor?"

She nodded, struggling not to cry. The paramedics were taking a scary length of time tending to Dalton, and while she didn't want to get in the way, she needed to talk to him, find out exactly what had happened.

Her cell phone rang, jarring her so sharply that she nearly jumped. She checked the display. Walker Nix. "Hello?"

"I just got a call about a knife attack in Edgewood. Someone said Dalton Hale was the victim—did he have Logan?"

"He did, but Logan's fine. I'm on scene."

"What about Hale?"

"He's hurt. I don't know how bad, but it doesn't seem immediately life threatening."

"We're on the way. Hang tight." Nix hung up.

Briar put her hand to her head, willing the pounding pulse in her ears to settle down to something approaching normal. "Thurman, I can't leave Logan—"

"No hurry now." His tone was kindly. Soothing. "You worry about your little fella. Backup's on the way."

One of the paramedics moved away from Dalton and approached her. She knew him from her time as a dispatcher—Clark Emerson. Nice guy. Doting father of three. He bent to look her in the eyes. "You two okay over here?"

"I think so. I didn't see any signs of injuries." She looked over at Dalton. "How's he?"

"It looks worse than it is. The wound is mostly superficial, though it cut through some muscle, so he's probably hurting a little. He needs stitches, but he doesn't want an ambulance. He wants to talk to you."

Briar glanced at her son. His sleepy-eyed gaze was on Dalton, who had pushed into a sitting position and was watching them as the other paramedic checked his vitals. "Come on, kiddo. Let's go talk to Mr. Hale." She scooped Logan up and carried him over to Dalton.

"How's he doing?" Dalton asked, lifting a hand toward Logan.

She crouched next to him, lowering Logan to his feet beside Dalton. Logan looked with interest at the blood-pressure cuff on Dalton's arm, peering more closely as the cuff began to expand.

"He's fine," she answered. "How about you?"

"I'm okay. Feeling a little embarrassed about nearly fainting from a little nick in the side."

The paramedic shushed them, forcing them to wait until he was finished with the blood-pressure check. "One-thirty over eighty," he murmured as he wrote it down.

"Is that good or bad?" Dalton asked.

"Not bad," the paramedic said with a smile.

Briar put her hand on Dalton's knee. "What happened?"

He looked down at her hand, then back at her. "I stopped for milk and cereal. Thought the little tiger here should have a decent breakfast in the morning. He picked Cheerios."

"His favorite." She managed a weak smile.

"We paid and went back out to the truck. Suddenly, the guy was just there. Dressed in dark clothes and he had this camouflage paint stuff on his face. And he had a knife."

"Do you know what kind of knife?"

"An enormous one." He shot her an apologetic look. "I'm useless as a witness, aren't I?"

"Maybe." Her smile was a little stronger this time. "But you faced down a man with a knife and kept my boy safe. So you're not going to hear any complaints from me."

"I'm sorry, Briar." He reached out and touched her hand where it lay on his knee. "I shouldn't have stopped for milk. I just didn't expect someone to strike in broad daylight, in public like this."

She hadn't, either. And the fact that the knife-wielding man had taken such a risky chance scared the hell out of her.

"WHY AREN'T YOU in an ambulance right now?"

Dalton dropped his hand from his aching head and turned at the sound of Doyle Massey's voice. Doyle had apparently come in on the heels of the detectives, who had pulled Briar aside for an update.

Dalton sighed. "I'm okay. I can drive myself to get stitched up."

"We'll need your shirt in case we can match the rip mark to a weapon."

"I know how evidence works," Dalton answered defensively.

Briar walked up, Logan on her hip, in time to hear his last words. "Then you know there's a chain of evidence that has to be maintained."

Doyle looked away from Dalton and frowned down at Briar. "Blackwood, you're on paid administrative leave until further notice."

Her brow furrowed as her eyes widened. "Sir?"

"What happened here isn't her fault," Dalton protested, reaching out to grab Doyle's arm. "This is my mistake.

I'll make sure it doesn't happen again. Please don't punish Briar for it."

Doyle's scowl disappeared and his gaze softened. "It's not punishment." He turned his gaze to Briar, his voice gentling. "You have a son to protect. You don't need to be leaving him with other people while you try to work. It'll be too much of a distraction."

Briar's chin came up, pride blazing in her cool gray eyes. "I don't want special treatment."

"I'm not giving you special treatment. Your son needs protection. So I'm assigning you to protect your son. This is your new job until we can figure out what's going on."

"Don't argue with him, Briar," Dalton murmured. "He's always right. Haven't you figured that out yet?"

Doyle snapped his head around to look at Dalton. "Not always. Sometimes people still manage to disappoint me no matter how low my expectations." He moved away to confer with Nix and Delilah Brand, the other Bitterwood detective who'd responded to the call.

"Don't you just love these family meetings?" Dalton murmured.

"You both seem to like gettin' a rise out of each other." Briar pressed her nose against Logan's hair and breathed deeply, as if breathing in the sweet, clean scent of him. "Dalton, I don't think I've said this properly—"

He jerked his head up, meeting her gaze with alarm. "Don't." He didn't want her to say thank you. He was damned lucky to have gotten away from the man with the knife. If the slightest thing had happened differently—he couldn't bear to think about what might have happened.

"You knocked the guy into a car with a half gallon of milk." Despite the haunted look in her eyes, her lips curved a bit at the sheer absurdity of his method of self-defense. "You got Logan to safety. While a guy was sticking an enormous knife in your side. If that's not heroic, I don't know what is."

"Technically, he swiped the knife. He didn't stick it," he corrected. "I'm not a hero, Briar. Anyone else would have done the same thing."

"You'd be surprised how few people would have done the same thing." She bent her head toward her son's soft curls again. "I hear he told you he'd let you go if you gave him Logan."

"I would never do that."

"I know. That's why I entrusted him to you in the first place." She looked up at him with shining eyes. The almost violent urge to wrap her and Logan up in his arms and never let them go caught him utterly flat-footed.

Nix's arrival kept him from doing something stupid. The detective looked at Briar with obvious affection, reaching out to palm the back of Logan's head. "The chief says if you want a ride back to the station, he's got room in his car." He looked at Dalton. "And if you'd like a ride to the hospital, he's offering that, as well. He'll stay with you and drop you back home when you're done."

Dalton looked past Nix and found Doyle leaning against the window near the door. His gaze met Dalton's and he gave a slight nod.

Oh, hell, Dalton thought. *Why not?* He needed a ride, and whether he liked it or not, the man was his brother. If the situation were reversed…

If the situation were reversed, he realized with some surprise, he'd do the same thing.

"I'll need your keys, Hale. To get Logan's car seat out of the truck."

Dalton handed off his keys. "Tell him I'll take the ride to the hospital."

Nix shot him an exasperated look. "For God's sake,

you're adults. Tell him yourself." He headed out to the parking lot.

"Are you sure you'll be okay going to the hospital alone with the chief?" Briar asked.

He slanted a look at her. "I'm a big boy."

"Remember to tell Doyle thank you."

Dalton laughed. "I'll try. It's a toss-up whether or not we'll make it to the hospital without killing each other."

"Do your best." She laid her hand on his arm, letting her fingers slide slowly down to his wrist before she let go. He barely controlled a shiver as her light touch sent tremors up and down his arm.

"Ready to go?" Doyle pushed away from the wall as they approached. He looked pointedly at Dalton. "Am I carting your butt to the hospital or what?"

"Your brotherly devotion is touching," Dalton murmured.

Doyle shot him a smart-alecky look, and Dalton realized he was getting to the point that he could predict the chief's reaction to his words.

Almost like a real brother.

IT WAS WELL after nine when Dalton finally called Briar to tell her he was coming up the front walkway. She hurried to unlock the door and let him in. She waved to Doyle, who waited in his police cruiser until Dalton was safely inside. "All stitched up?"

He nodded. "Want to see my wound?"

Smiling, she shook her head. "You hungry? Logan and I had chicken soup for dinner. I can heat some up for you."

He caught her hand as she moved toward the kitchen, his fingers warm and firm around hers. "Doyle and I grabbed a burger on the way home."

"How'd that go?" She waited for him to let go of her

hand, but he twined his fingers with hers instead, leading her over to the sofa. He sat heavily, tugging her down beside him.

"It went…better than I expected. He wasn't a complete smart-ass, and I tried not to be a defensive jerk. So…progress." He gave her hand a light squeeze. "Logan asleep?"

She looked down at their twined hands, her gaze drawn by the intersection of her fair skin and his tanned fingers. "About thirty minutes ago. We had to read a couple of extra stories, and he was worried that you weren't home yet, but I explained you had to go somewhere with your brother. I also promised you'd look in on him before you go to bed. You don't have to, though. Once he falls asleep, it takes a bulldozer to wake him. He wouldn't know you were there."

"I'll know," he said, turning his head toward her.

She met his gaze, a ripple of pure feminine awareness rolling through her, setting off a dozen tingles along her spine. Despite the weariness in his eyes, the faint pallor beneath his healthy tan, he was still one of the most attractive men she'd ever seen.

Man *being the operative word,* she thought as she drowned a little in his warm green gaze. He was a man, flaws and all, in a way Johnny never had been. Though she was still in her twenties, giving birth to Logan had changed her from a girl to a woman almost overnight.

But was she woman enough to deal with a man like Dalton? A man who'd lived a life of privilege she couldn't even begin to imagine, much less understand? A man with his own demons that made her day-to-day struggles seem like bumps in the road in comparison?

She'd worked hard over the past few months to simplify her life, to focus her attention completely on her son and his future. Letting herself get involved with another person had never figured into her plans.

But she knew, with a certainty that sent heat blazing into the center of her sex, if he dipped his head closer, she would close the distance between them and take whatever he chose to offer.

"Last night," he murmured, "I wanted to kiss you."

She closed her eyes, overwhelmed by his raw honesty. "I know."

"I still do."

She opened her eyes and leaned closer, even as her self-protective instincts screamed at her to get up and walk away. "It's a bad idea."

"It really is."

She brushed her fingertips against his chest, tracing the contours of his muscles. He was well built for a man who worked in an office, with lean, defined muscles. He kept himself fit.

"Do you know why I never called Lydia back today?" he asked, his gaze dropping to her mouth.

"Because you're a heel?" she asked, her own gaze sliding over his mouth, noting—not for the first time—the tempting fullness of his lower lip.

That lower lip curved upward at the corners in response to her remark. "I suppose I can't deny it, can I? You saw the whole scene play out."

"You should have told her the truth."

His eyes flickered up away from her mouth, and his gaze leveled with hers. "I don't think she'd have liked the truth all that much."

"Which was?" she prodded, knowing she was playing with wildfire.

"That I forgot all about her the minute I saw you that first night at the hospital." He dipped his head toward her. "You're all I seem to think about. How to keep you safe. How to protect Logan. Whether I can do it or not."

He always seemed so confident and controlled. To hear him express uncertainty was a sobering experience. "What a messy situation you've gotten yourself into."

His lips twitched upward again. "I have a knack for it these days."

"How was lunch with your mother?"

He lifted one dark eyebrow. "How'd you hear about that?"

"I tried to call you around lunchtime but you were out. Your secretary mentioned you were having lunch with your mother." She couldn't stop herself from snuggling a little closer. "How is she holding up?"

"Better than I thought she would." He sighed, leaning away from her and laying his head back on the sofa cushions. "They were so wrong about her, you know. My father and grandfather. They claim they were protecting her, but she's so much stronger than either of them gave her credit for."

"How long has it been since you spoke to your dad?" Briar asked.

He rolled his head toward her. "Why?"

"I lost my daddy when I was ten. I wish I could talk to him now."

He reached out to touch her cheek, grimacing as the movement apparently pulled on his stitches. He fell back, gazing up at the ceiling.

If she'd been thinking more clearly, she probably would have gotten up right then and headed up to bed. But the night had been nearly as harrowing for her as it had been for him. And she wasn't quite ready for it to end.

Slowly, she lifted her hand to his face, cupping the curve of his jaw. His gaze slid down to meet hers, the green of his eyes warm and liquid, like a mossy mountain pool.

"I'm going to kiss you," she whispered. "It doesn't have to mean anything you don't want it to mean."

His hand sliding up her back to tangle in her hair, he pulled her toward him, his breath hot against her cheek. She angled her lips across his, a light exploratory touch. Dry, warm, closed-mouth. Almost chaste.

Almost.

His lips parted under hers, the slick heat of his tongue brushing over her bottom lip, teasing it lightly at first, then with a demanding intensity that shook her to her suddenly burning core.

And any thought of chastity went right out the window.

Chapter Ten

Briar straddled Dalton's thighs, sliding forward until he felt the soft heat of her sex settle flush against his growing hardness, flesh separated from flesh by a couple of layers of clothing. The sensation rocketed straight to his brain, exploding like fireworks and spreading molten pleasure to every part of his body. Convulsively tightening his trembling fingers in her tangle of curls, he flattened his other hand against the small of her back, urging her hips forward to increase the delicious friction building between their bodies.

He nuzzled his way down the curve of her throat, his lips brushing lightly over her skin. He kissed the skin beneath her jaw, the delicate curve of her chin, then lightly nipped his way back up to her mouth.

Her lips parting beneath the pressure of his own, she surged toward him, flattening her breasts against his chest. Her fingers skimmed his rib cage through his shirt, exploring the ridges as if seeking to map every contour. Her actions sparked a fresh surge of heat through his blood and fire along the path her fingers traveled, until his whole body felt on the verge of combustion. He didn't even care when her gentle touches tugged the still-tender skin of his wounded side.

Somewhere in the depths of his desire-addled brain, he

knew what they were doing was a mistake. But he couldn't seem to quell the primal urge to bury his hardness in her soft heat, and her sweet, fierce response to his touch drove out what remained of his good sense.

So easy, he thought. So easy to bury himself inside her and forget about everything else. Forget the tatters of his life. The danger gathering like a firestorm outside the walls of their sensual cocoon.

So easy to drop his guard.

Just as he'd dropped it earlier tonight in the parking lot.

With another groan, he dragged his mouth from hers, his breath coming in harsh, rapid gasps. He caught her hips in both hands and moved her carefully away from his own hips. "Briar, this isn't a good idea."

She dropped her head forward, let it fall against his shoulder. Her curls whispered against his cheeks. "I know."

For a long moment, they just breathed together, hitching, syncopated gasps that slowly ebbed into gentle sighs. Finally, she rolled away from his lap, slumping back against the sofa cushions. "I'm sorry," she said.

Her words surprised him so much that he couldn't stop a soft huff of laughter. "For what?"

"For…that."

He couldn't quite stop himself from teasing her a little. "For riding me like a cowgirl in a rodeo?"

She flashed him a look that made him laugh a little harder.

"Come on, Briar. We're adults. No harm done, right?"

Except he wasn't so sure about that, was he? He wasn't a man prone to indulging his body's urges without consideration and thought. His control, in fact, was damned near legendary, leading more than one woman he'd dated to accuse him of having ice in his veins instead of blood.

But no ice could have survived the flood of fire that

had swamped his body at Briar's touch. He didn't know why she had evoked such an uncharacteristic response in him, but he couldn't deny it had happened. And he had a bad feeling that if he gave it too much more thought, he wouldn't find the answer reassuring.

But whatever his reason for losing control, he was certain of one thing: he would be a fool to let it happen again.

"I wasn't expecting that," she ventured after another moment of silence. "I don't— This isn't something I do. You know?"

"I wasn't expecting it, either," he admitted.

"I know it's the twenty-first century and women are free to embrace their sexuality, but…" Her gaze lifted, finally, and settled on his face. "I just don't do this."

"Believe it or not, neither do I. Not out of the blue this way." He hadn't meant to admit that fact to her. He could have shrugged it off with jaded humor, as if he went about seducing women every day. Better than admit that her touch had damned near unraveled him.

"So we agree?" she asked.

He gave her a wary look. "About what?"

"That we don't need to do this again."

What he needed, he thought, barely tamping down a shudder of raw need, was to strip off those snug little jeans of hers and sink into the softness hidden between her sleek thighs. That's what he needed.

Aloud, however, he said, "Agreed." He pushed himself up from the sofa and looked down at her. "I need some sleep. I bet you do, too."

She stared up at him, her eyes dark and liquid. The urge to seduce her all over again, to take her up to his bedroom and finish what they'd started, damned near overwhelmed him once more.

But she rose to her feet with steady, unhurried dignity

and took a step away from him. "If you'll make sure the alarm is set, I'll check all the locks."

Working in silent accord, they kept their distance from each other as they fortified their defenses against the danger outside. But as Dalton found his gaze straying toward Briar's slim figure over and over, he realized there might be no way to defend himself against the unexpected danger of Briar Blackwood living under his roof.

TWILIGHT CAST A deep indigo gloom over the convenience store parking lot, broken only by the flash of cherry lights spinning atop the fire department emergency bus. A crowd had gathered, vultures circling a fresh kill. They stood in a writhing knot of anticipation near a pickup truck parked not far from the store entrance.

Briar made her way through the throbbing mass of on-lookers, her pulse racing so frantically that she couldn't make out individual beats, just a cacophony of terror building to incessant white noise in her ears.

The crowd seemed to go on for miles, rolling around her like waves in the ocean, prolonging the dread. But finally, she reached the center of the throng to look upon the spectacle that had drawn them.

He lay facedown on the dirty parking lot pavement, utterly still. Beneath him a river of red spread in lightly undulating waves, the ripples slowly dying away to nothing, the memory of his life pulse fading into stillness.

She tore her gaze away and looked at the ground beside him. A torn bag lay next to him, spilling its contents on the edge of his pooling blood. A jug of milk. A box of cereal. Both stained red.

And beside the torn shopping bag, a turtle-shaped backpack, straps severed, as if someone had ripped it off the little boy who'd worn it.

"No," she moaned, but the words felt as if they stuck in her aching throat. She crouched beside the fallen warrior, heedless of the blood staining her hands. "Please, please—" She lifted a shaking hand to his pale face, touched his cold cheek.

His eyes snapped open. "Briar?"

She jarred awake, her heart rat-a-tatting against her breastbone. It was still dark outside, the only light coming from the open doorway.

In the rectangle of light from the hall, Dalton's tall muscular silhouette stood over her. "I'm sorry to wake you," he said quietly, glancing at the sleeping little boy by her side. "I have to leave for a while."

She squinted at the travel alarm she'd set on the bedside table. Not even six yet. "What's wrong?"

"It's my father," he answered. "He had some sort of attack. He's in the hospital in Maryville."

She pushed her tangled hair out of her face, the jangling sensation in her sleep-addled brain finally subsiding. "How bad?"

"He's stable, but nobody's been able to give me any information beyond that. I just didn't want you to wake up and wonder where I'd gone. And maybe we should call Nix or someone to come stay with you?"

"No need to bother Nix. Those hillbillies can't get to me here the way they can out in the woods. And if they try, well, I'm armed and lookin' for a little payback." She pushed off the covers and rolled to a sitting position on the edge of the bed, relieved she'd decided to wear sweats to bed the night before. Of course, considering how close they'd come to getting naked together the night before, her attack of modesty was a little tardy. "Have you eaten anything?"

"No, but—"

She stood and wrapped her hand firmly around his arm, nudging him toward the door. "You can't go to Maryville hungry. Not in your condition."

He didn't protest as she led him downstairs to the kitchen. He even sat quietly at the breakfast bar and let her take over. She darted a look at him as she searched the cabinets for his cookware, seeing in the glare of the kitchen light what the shadows of his bedroom had hidden.

He was in emotional shock.

She put down the frying pan she'd just retrieved and crossed to the bar, reaching for his hands. They were cool to the touch.

His haunted green eyes rose to meet hers. "I told him I was ashamed I'd ever called him my father. That's the last thing I said to him."

She tightened her grip on his hands. "So tell him you made a mistake."

"What if he's—"

"You just said he's stable."

"That could change. It could change before I get there." He looked down at their clasped hands. "Briar, he could die before I get there."

She wished she could go with him. Give him the moral support her friends had given her that night as she waited for word on her aunt's condition. But she had to stay with Logan.

"Let me call somebody to go with you," she suggested.

His gaze snapped up to meet hers. "There's no one. Mother can't—I don't want her there until I know more."

"There's your brother. Or your sister."

He closed his eyes. "I haven't exactly given them any reason to want to hold my hand through this mess."

"Family doesn't need a reason."

The vulnerability in his eyes when they met hers made her heart ache. "I can't ask them."

Maybe not, she thought.

But she could.

"IT WASN'T A HEART ATTACK." The E.R. doctor had introduced himself as Dr. Treadway. He was a short stocky man in his early forties with thinning hair and a kind smile. "His blood pressure was elevated when he came into the E.R. and his heart rate was up. He was hyperventilating a bit, but we were able to get that under control with a sedative. We're doing more tests to be sure, but the signs are pointing to an anxiety attack."

Dalton covered his eyes with his hand for a moment, his body tingling with relief. "Can I see him?"

"There's a guard posted outside his room. You'll have to clear it with him."

Of course. His father was still a prisoner. The judge in Barrowville had refused to set bail, considering Paul Hale a flight risk and a potential danger to Dana Massey.

But he didn't look like a dangerous man, lying pale and groggy in the hospital bed. The guard turned out to be a man Dalton had met several times in his job as a prosecutor. He'd allowed Dalton into the room without protest.

Paul Hale turned his head at the sound of Dalton's footsteps approaching the bed. Color flushed through his cheeks, driving out the pallor. "I didn't expect to see you."

Dalton pulled up a nearby chair. "I didn't expect to be here."

"They say I'll live."

"I'm glad."

Paul's gaze narrowed. "Are you?"

"I'm sorry about what I said to you before."

"Which thing? You said a lot of things."

Dalton felt a flurry of anger beating in his chest like bats flushed out of the dark bowels of a cavern. "You tried to shoot my sister."

His father's gaze snapped up to meet his. "Your sister."

"That's what she is." The words flowed easily over his tongue, surprising him. But he felt a glimmer of freedom in saying the words aloud.

"I've never heard you call her that."

"I haven't called her that before."

His father's expression shifted to curiosity. "Why now?"

"I guess because I've had enough time to accept the truth of it. She's my sister. Doyle Massey is my brother. Tallie Cumberland gave birth to me." *And your father-in-law stole me from her and gave me to you and your wife. And then made sure Tallie didn't live to tell me the truth.*

"Tallie Cumberland wasn't your mother."

"She wasn't given the chance to be."

Paul shifted restlessly in the hospital bed, the movement rattling the cuff chaining him to the bed. "That was your grandfather's doing."

"I'm aware of that."

"Have you talked to the old man?"

Dalton shook his head. "I don't expect to. He's not talking to anyone but his lawyer."

"How's your mother? Does she know?"

"About your being here? No. I'll call her later this morning to let her know."

"Don't let her come here. I don't want her to see me this way."

"She knows you're in jail. Seeing you shackled to the bed won't come as a surprise."

"She trusted me to be her protector. Her rock."

And he'd failed her, Dalton thought, trying not to think of his own near failure the night before. Trying not to remember how close he'd come to letting the man with the knife rip Briar Blackwood's life into shreds.

"I can't stay here long," he said, reaching out to straighten the rumpled edge of the sheet covering his father.

"Late for work?" His father's tone wavered between self-pity and a hint of admiration. Paul Hale had been enormously proud of Dalton's work as a prosecutor. Ironic, really, given his current state of legal woes.

"I'm working from home today." He didn't elaborate. He didn't quite trust his father enough to share Briar's problems with him, or his own part in trying to keep her and her son alive. "But I have things to attend to."

"I see." His father's chin lifted, vestiges of the old Hale pride evident in the set of his jaw and the steely coolness of his eyes.

"I'll visit you when you're out of here."

"Back in jail, you mean."

Dalton sighed, more disappointed than angry at his father. Progress, he supposed. "You did a terrible thing. Regardless of your motives, you could have killed Dana. She didn't do a damned thing to deserve it."

"She was going to rip us apart. She *has* ripped us apart."

"Grandfather ripped us apart. With your help." Dalton rose to his feet, needing to leave this room, to breathe something besides the poison of his father's self-pity. "I'll see you soon. I hope you continue feeling better."

"I love you." Paul's voice followed him to the door.

Dalton paused in the doorway, turning slowly. "I love you, too. Dad," he said.

And meant it.

In the hall, two people were waiting. They looked up at him warily through green eyes very like his own.

"Briar called us," Dana Massey said, breaking the tense silence. "She said to tell you she was sorry for interfering."

"But not sorry enough not to do it?" He wasn't angry with her, he realized. He was actually rather glad to see his brother and sister waiting for him. Otherwise, he might be feeling pretty damned alone about now.

"If you want us to go, we'll go," Doyle said. "But we thought you should at least have the option of having someone here with you for this."

"I don't want you to go," Dalton admitted.

Dana lifted one hand to his arm, her touch tentative. "There's a good coffee shop down the street from here. I discovered it when Doyle was in the hospital after his truck flipped."

The accident his grandfather had caused, Dalton thought with grim dismay. But neither Doyle nor his sister seemed inclined to hold him responsible for his family's crimes.

They had treated him far more kindly than he'd treated them.

He covered her hand with his, giving it a light squeeze before he let go. It wasn't much, he supposed, as far as brotherly affection went. But it wasn't nothing, either.

"You'll pay, right?" Doyle asked, shooting him a grin.

Dalton couldn't stop a laugh.

"Younger brothers," Dana murmured as they fell in step, heading for the elevators. "Such mooches."

Brothers and sisters, Dalton thought as he followed them into the elevator alcove. He guessed he had to get used to having them.

Chapter Eleven

Waiting for Dalton to return had proved a more nerve-racking experience than Briar had expected. She'd been afraid he'd changed his mind about working from home and had gone to the office to get as far from her as he could. But a call to his secretary had established that he hadn't gone in to the office.

Neither had he called, not once in the four hours since he'd left the house. The drive to Maryville took twenty minutes. Had he stayed with his father the rest of the time?

Had his father's condition deteriorated?

She had tried to fill the hours with the business of Johnny's murder and how it might tie into the recent threats against her and her son. He'd died months ago. So why had it taken Blake and his cohort this long to make a move? Had something changed?

Dalton had changed, she realized with a flash of insight. The upheaval in his personal life had led him to attack the Cortland crime organization investigation with additional zeal. She wasn't certain of the timeline, but he'd spoken of the lumber yard bookkeeper he'd interrogated as if she was a recent contact. A new lead in the investigation.

Dalton had been the catalyst.

It was possible, even likely, that Blake had learned of the new lead, as well. She knew Wayne Cortland's band of rogues had included people with access to the Bitter-wood P.D. Probably the county sheriff's department, as well. Maybe even the Ridge County prosecutor's office. If Dalton suspected Johnny had stolen something valuable from Wayne Cortland by way of his affair with Cortland's bookkeeper, then her cousin probably suspected it, too.

The rattle of the front-door knob sent a corresponding echo through her taut nerves. Her hand closed around the butt of her Glock, relaxing only when she saw Dalton walk through the open doorway.

He paused midstride when his gaze met hers.

"Are you angry at me?" she blurted, though it hadn't been the question she'd planned.

He shook his head. "I had coffee with my brother and sister." A fleeting look of wonder crossed his face. "Never thought I'd say that." He locked the door behind him and crossed to the sofa, dropping heavily onto the soft cushions. He looked so tired, Briar thought, her own muscles aching with sympathy. "Where's Logan?"

"He's napping."

Dalton looked at his watch. "At ten-thirty?"

She sat in the chair across from him, not quite trust-ing herself to sit beside him again so soon after their loss of control the night before. "Last night was a lot of ex-citement for a little boy. He didn't sleep well." She hadn't even had to try hard to coax him into taking an early nap. "How's your father?"

"He's going to be fine. The doctor is pretty sure it was a panic attack."

"I'm glad to hear it." She let herself breathe again. "Did you see him?"

"I saw him." He passed his hand over his face, as if he could wipe away the weariness lining his face. "I don't sup-pose I've ever actually thought about my father in terms of strength or weakness. I think we assume our parents are either saints or demons, you know?"

"We see what we want to," she murmured.

"Or what we need to."

"I think that's probably true of most people in our lives." She thought about Johnny, about the lies she'd fed herself with the willingness of a young girl in love for the first time. "We look past the flaws and oversell the good parts."

His green eyes met hers, understanding passing across the space between them through that electric clash of gazes. "My father feels sorry for himself. He can't quite let himself come to terms with his failures. He needs to blame someone else."

"That's pretty human," she said gently.

"It is." He gave a brief nod. "But it's not particularly admirable."

"Have you always done the admirable thing since learning the truth about your birth?"

He looked down at his hands, his brow folding into a grim scowl. "God, no."

"The truth can be a real cold bitch," she murmured.

"You said you knew Johnny had been cheating on you," he said after a few moments of awkward silence. "When did it start?"

"The cheating?" She thought about it, even though the stark truth was painful even now. "I don't know. I had made him wait until we were married to have sex. And he seemed so patient about it, even though I knew he wanted me. But now I wonder..."

"You think he wasn't really being patient at all?"

"I grew up with Johnny. I'd been crazy about him since I was old enough to realize just what the difference between boys and girls really meant. When we started dating, I was utterly determined that he was the man I'd marry someday. And I was right." She couldn't stop a little smile at the memory of her happiness when Johnny had asked her to marry him. She had seen that moment as the beginning of her future. And it had been, though not quite in the way she'd foreseen.

She gripped her knees to keep her restless hands still. "We were both eighteen when we married. Young, though not so young compared to our parents' generation. Johnny already had a good job driving trucks for a mining company, and I had started as a dispatcher with Bitterwood Emergency Services. We thought we had our lives all figured out. We wanted babies. Lots of babies. But that didn't work out so well, either."

He looked at her oddly. "But Logan—is he adopted?"

"No, he's my biological son," she said quickly. "Johnny wouldn't consider adoption. And we probably couldn't have afforded it even if he'd thought differently. I think he wanted a child to prove something."

"Prove what?"

"I don't know. You're a man. You tell me."

"Some men see it as proof of virility," he said after a moment. "Like they're real men if they can plant their seed somewhere." Dalton didn't sound as if he agreed. "I wonder if my father felt that way. If that's why he covered up the truth about me."

"He saw you as his son. For a lot of years, he didn't know you weren't. Biologically, I mean."

"Biology," he murmured. "Just a bunch of nucleotides on a double helix, and yet it seems to rule our destinies."

"God, I hope not," she said. "I'm a Culpepper by birth, remember."

He looked up with a smile. "Not all Culpeppers are bad, are they?"

She gave a rueful laugh. "Depends on who you ask, I reckon."

"I guess Johnny was thrilled when you got pregnant with Logan?"

"Over the moon," she admitted, smiling at first until she remembered the months and years leading up to that brief moment of sheer joy. "I thought everything was going to be better then."

"Better than what?"

She realized that she was spilling her deepest, darkest secrets to a man she'd barely known by sight just a few days earlier. How had she let herself become so vulnerable?

And why did the thought not scare her more than it did?

"I'm sorry," he said a moment later as she continued to hesitate. "I'm asking a lot of personal questions that are none of my business."

"Johnny's personality seemed to change when we kept trying to have a baby and couldn't," she said, making herself ignore his tacit offer to change the subject. She'd kept Johnny's secrets for years, preventing his friends, his family and especially her own family from seeing the growing cracks in their young marriage.

But there was no marriage to protect any longer. And Johnny had been dead for a while now. The secrets burned in her gut like acid, and maybe it was time to get them out of her system before they destroyed her.

"At first we just thought it was bad luck. Bad timing. We started reading books about things like ovulation and biological timetables. It was a lark at first. We laughed about it a lot. Johnny had never been a big reader, but he tackled those books like they were instructional manuals." She laughed aloud at the memory. "We'd make naughty jokes about screws and nails and putting the right tabs into the right slots."

Dalton's smile almost made it to his eyes.

"But when all the reading and all the jokes and all the sex never produced a baby, he stopped smiling about it." The mood change had been palpable, she remembered. Joy had become dread. Sex had ceased to be communication and became instead an act of desperation. "We couldn't afford fertility treatments or expensive tests, and I sometimes wonder if he didn't prefer it that way. Easier to blame me than himself. And if we couldn't test to see who was really to blame—"

"Then he could keep believing it wasn't his fault."

"It wasn't anyone's fault. That's not how it works. Nature gives us what it gives us, and assigning blame about it is stupid and cruel."

"My parents tried forever to have a baby, without luck. When they had me—" Dalton stopped, a rueful grimace of a smile touching his lips as he started again. "When they had their son, they considered it a miracle."

"I guess your grandfather didn't want to rip that miracle away from them," she said. "When the baby died."

"I guess so. But his motives don't excuse his actions."

"No."

He looked up at her, raw emotion burning in his green eyes. "I don't know how to feel about any of it. It's like I woke up one day, looked in the mirror and saw a stranger."

"You're the same person," she said quietly, wanting desperately to cross the space between them and take him in her arms. Comfort the lost little boy that stared out from those pain-filled eyes. But she didn't trust herself to stop with comfort. "It's the world around you that's changed."

"Then maybe I need to quit whining and just get on with changing myself to adapt?"

She smiled. "I think I'd have put it more delicately."

He laughed. "You're a lot of things, Briar Blackwood,

but delicate is not one of them." After a moment, when she didn't join in the laughter, he added, "That's a good thing, you know. Delicate things end up trampled to dust sooner or later. In my line of work, I've seen it happen too often."

"You can't afford to be soft living in the mountains," she said. "You have to be tough, or the hills will eat you alive."

He gave her a thoughtful look. "I guess this would be a bad time, then, to suggest you and Logan should leave Bitterwood."

She stared at him, her mind rebelling against the thought. Life in these mountains had been hard, just as she'd said. Painful at times. But the mountains were her home. She'd carved a life out of these rocks and trees and smoky hills, and she didn't want to leave this place in fear.

"I have a friend who lives in Colorado. In the mountains. It's beautiful there, especially during the snowy season. You and Logan could learn to ski. Or snowboard. No one would find you there."

"You think we should run away? Leave everyone we know?"

He looked down at his hands for a long moment before his gaze snapped up, blazing with raw energy. "I could go with you. You're right about the world around me being different. So maybe it's the perfect time to change my world on purpose. Go somewhere, start fresh."

"With me?" She couldn't believe that was what he was suggesting.

"I don't know," he admitted, finally looking away. She felt a strange sort of relief not having those burning eyes gazing into her as if he could read the secrets of her soul. At the same time, she felt as if a cord connecting them for a brief electric moment had snapped, leaving her floating in some cold and lonely void. Her head ached with confusion.

"I'm not finished fighting," she said when it was clear

he'd say nothing more. "Not yet. We don't even know what we're looking for, do we? Blake seems determined to get some sort of leverage over me before he even tells me what he wants."

"That reminds me. I stopped by the office on the way home to pick up some files I had copied for you, but I left them in the car. Be right back." He went outside and came back in a minute with a large manila file folder stuffed with papers. "Come over here and I'll go through them with you," he suggested, laying the folder on the coffee table and sitting on the sofa, making room for her to join him.

She settled beside him on the sofa, allowing herself the small pleasure of his solid warmth against her side, even though their bodies didn't quite touch. "This is a lot of information," she said, unable to contain her surprise. It was certainly more information than the Bitterwood P.D. seemed to have on the Cortland organization.

"I have access to a lot of jurisdictions, even outside Tennessee," Dalton told her. "I've tried to organize things into the groups we think are working together." Within the file folder, she saw, he'd divided the papers into sections. One section was labeled Police Agencies. Another bore the label Anarchists/Antigovernment Radicals. A third was called Meth/Pot/Oxy. That, Briar supposed, would be all they'd gathered on the hodgepodge of drug cookers, pot growers and narcotics dealers Cortland had used as informants and sometimes hired killers to do his dirty work.

The fourth section, labeled Militias, was thinner than the others, Briar saw with some dismay. Even calling it Militias in the plural was clearly a bit of wish casting, for everything inside that section of Dalton's notes was about one particular militia—the Blue Ridge Infantry.

"What do you know about the BRI?" Dalton asked.

"It started with a little moonshine and a whole lot of bitterness," she answered slowly, thinking back on the stories she'd heard from her mother, a woman with little love for any Culpeppers beyond her own husband and children. "I don't know how well versed in mountain genealogy you folks here on the Edgewood side of town are, but there are Culpeppers up and down these hills from Alabama to the Maryland state line. And about thirty-five years ago, some of the Culpeppers got sucked into the militia movement. Now, some of them had fairly honorable reasons for it. They thought the government was getting too big for its britches, and it was up to regular folks to remind the government just who served who."

"That's not the Blue Ridge Infantry's goal at the moment," Dalton countered.

"No, it's not. And that's why you'll find a whole lot of folks round here who'd just as soon spit on the ground the BRI walks on as anything. Some of the militia members left started using the whole 'government is the devil' excuse to run moonshine, cook meth, grow pot—anything they could call government overreach, they made it into a BRI cause."

"How did Blake Culpepper get involved?"

"He's like a lot of folks in these hills. Chip on his shoulder the size of Chimney Rock. Thinks the world owes him something better than he has, but he's not willing to work for it." She shook her head, pressing her mouth flat as if to suppress the anger rising in her chest. "Or maybe he just likes hurtin' people. Seems like he works hard enough doin' bad when he's looking to make life miserable for somebody else."

"Did he and Johnny ever have reason to cross paths?"

"Sure. Johnny grew up here. On our side of the tracks, you don't get to pick and choose your neighbors. Or lock yourself up inside some gate."

He gave her a thoughtful look that made her feel churlish for having said what she had. Maybe Blake wasn't the only one with a chip on his shoulder.

"Johnny liked everybody, and he wasn't one to judge. He once told me that if he had to cut people out of his life for breaking the law, he wouldn't have any friends left." She flipped through the list of names Dalton had compiled, names of men and women the prosecutor's office believed were connected, either directly or indirectly, to the BRI.

"We went to school with half the people on this list. Went to church with some of 'em. Johnny probably played football with several." With a sigh, she pushed the folder away, feeling tired and out of sync with the world around her, as if there was no place that felt like home anymore.

"What could Johnny have taken that would be worth terrorizing you to get?" Dalton asked.

"I've been thinking about that all morning, ever since you left. And the only thing that seems clear is that you're the catalyst that set everything into motion."

Dalton's dark eyebrow rose. "I'm the catalyst?"

"Johnny died months ago. But nobody gave me a minute's worry until just a few days ago. Why? What happened a few days ago to make Blake and his crew think Johnny had given me something incriminating?"

Dalton's brow furrowed.

"Why did you come to the hospital that night? Why would you do that?" she asked.

"Because I thought—" He stopped short, looking down at the file, the creases in his forehead deepening.

"You thought I might know something about what Johnny took from Wayne Cortland."

His gaze snapped up to meet hers.

"Why did you think that?" she asked. "Because you

found out Johnny had been having an affair with Cortland's former bookkeeper?"

"That was part of it," he admitted.

"But there was more?"

He looked down at the file again, a pained look on his face as if he knew something he didn't want to tell her.

"For God's sake, Dalton. I'm not going to crumble if you tell me something unpleasant about Johnny."

He took a long deep breath and slowly met her gaze. "She said he liked to take risks."

A finger of dread scraped its way down her spine, trailing cold tremors. "What kind of risks?"

"Like sneaking her into Cortland's office for sex."

She looked at Dalton through narrowed eyes, almost feeling sorry for him. She could see how much he disliked having to say such things to her, his regret etched in fine lines and dark shadows all over his face. "They had sex in Cortland's office? With Cortland there in the building?"

"I don't know. I didn't ask for details."

"Maybe you should have." An idea began to form, one she didn't particularly want to have. One, in fact, that she dreaded intensely.

But it made a grim sort of sense. And it just might give them the answers they were looking for.

"Tell me where I can find the Cortland bookkeeper," she said after a long, tense silence. "I want to meet her."

Chapter Twelve

Working as a bookkeeper for a now-notorious crime boss couldn't have given Leanne Dawson much of a career boost, Briar thought as she walked across the gravel parking lot in front of Pinter Construction in Wytheville, Virginia. The building housing the offices was a small cinder-block structure once painted a sunny yellow that had long since faded into a dusty dun color. The name Pinter Construction was barely legible in peeling blue paint over the front door.

Inside, there were no cubicles, only a central desk at the front and a handful of desks lining the walls. Most of those were unoccupied, save for one near the back, occupied by a dark-haired man in his forties who was typing something in a series of painfully slow pecks, and another on the right-hand wall where a slim blonde was writing something onto a notepad from time to time as she consulted a book lying open on her desk.

At the front desk, a pretty dark-haired girl in her early twenties had her cell phone perched on her very pregnant stomach and didn't even acknowledge Briar's entrance.

Briar stepped up to the reception desk. "Is Leanne Dawson here?"

The pregnant girl looked up in surprise. "I'm sorry, what?"

"I need to speak to Leanne Dawson. Is she here?" For a brief dizzying moment, it occurred to her that this girl could be Leanne. And if she was pregnant—

But to her relief, the dark-haired girl just waved a hand in the general direction of the slim blonde on the right. "She's over there."

No offer to let her know Briar was coming. Which, she supposed, might work in her favor.

She crossed to the desk where the blonde continued jotting down notes, her hair covering her face like a curtain. Briar cleared her throat, making the woman jump.

"Leanne Dawson?" she asked.

The woman swept the shiny blond curtain away from her face, giving Briar a good look at the woman her husband had been sleeping with.

She was a pretty woman and, to Briar's bemusement, at least five years older than Briar herself, with clear blue eyes and lightly tanned skin that contrasted pleasantly with her straight wheat-colored hair. She was slim but well proportioned, with full breasts and long legs, displayed modestly enough by her tailored blouse and well-cut slacks.

"I'm Leanne Dawson. May I help you?"

Her accent was Southern but light and well modulated. An educated woman who hadn't lived in the hills her whole life, Briar thought. Had that been part of the attraction for Johnny, beyond Leanne's position as Cortland's bookkeeper? Had he enjoyed being with someone so obviously different from the little hillbilly girl back home?

Stop it, she scolded herself silently.

"My name is Briar Culpepper." She wondered as she gave her maiden name whether or not Johnny had told Leanne Dawson anything about the wife back home. If he had, Leanne showed no sign of recognition. "I'm a police officer in Bitterwood, Tennessee, looking into the murder of John Blackwood."

Leanne's expression shifted at the mention of Johnny's name. Bleakness darkened the blue of her eyes, and her lower lip trembled slightly as she waved at an empty folding chair on the other side of her desk. As Briar took a seat, Leanne said quietly, "I don't know anything about his death."

"But you knew John Blackwood."

"We were…friends."

"You were a little more than friends," Briar pressed, feeling pretty terrible for pushing the other woman this way without revealing the truth about herself. And if Logan's life hadn't been at stake, she probably would have come clean and asked for the woman's forbearance. But she couldn't afford to alienate Leanne Dawson until she asked the questions she wanted answered.

"Officer—"

"Call me Briar."

"Pretty name." Leanne smiled slightly before the expression faded into gloom again. "I've talked to so many people about him. I don't know what more to say. I made a really awful mistake. Not just where Johnny was concerned, either."

"I understand from your earlier statement to Ridge County prosecutor Dalton Hale that you and Johnny engaged in your liaisons in Wayne Cortland's office."

Beneath her tan, Leanne blushed deep pink, making Briar feel like a complete creep. "Only a few times."

"Did you go into the office together always? Or was Johnny ever alone there without you?"

Leanne's gaze darted up to meet Briar's. "Why?"

"We're trying to establish if Mr. Blackwood ever had access to Cortland's office unattended."

Leanne licked her lips, looking down at the open ledger that lay on the desk in front of her. As if suddenly realizing the company's books were laid bare to Briar if she wanted to look, she snapped the book closed and folded her hands on top of the book. "I made the mistake of giving Johnny liberties I shouldn't have."

"Including allowing him to go into Wayne Cortland's office unescorted? Maybe to wait until you could safely sneak away?"

Leanne lowered her face to her hands. "He made it seem so exciting. Fun and dangerous." She dropped her hands and looked at Briar, her expression stiff with embarrassment. "I don't attract exciting, dangerous men. He made me feel so alive."

Briar felt a hard, hot ache in the center of her chest, but to her surprise, it had less to do with her own feeling of betrayal and more to do with her sympathy for Leanne Dawson's obvious sense of shame and regret.

"So he made a game of your relationship. And part of that game was doing something crazy and dangerous. Like having sex in your boss's office?"

She nodded, a tear sliding down her cheek. "Sometimes it would take a half hour to get away. I was so afraid Mr. Cortland would go in there and find Johnny, my heart would be beating a mile a minute by the time—" She stopped, dashing the tear from her face with an angry stab of her knuckle. "All that time, he had a wife and I didn't know it. I guess that's what made it feel dangerous for him, huh?"

Briar looked down at her own hands, at the faint ring of pale skin on her left ring finger where the ring had been until Johnny's death. "Did Mr. Cortland have a safe? Or a drawer or file cabinet nobody else was allowed to access?" she asked.

"You know, that prosecutor asked me the same question, but I didn't remember—" Leanne paused, then started again. "It might not have meant anything. But there was a drawer in Mr. Cortland's desk that he used to always keep locked. Not that unusual—he might have kept personal items there. People do, you know. But just the other day, I remembered that he stopped locking the drawer a few months before the explosion."

The explosion that had blown Wayne Cortland to his eternal reward, Briar thought, along with several other people, some of whom may have been innocent pawns in Cortland's games. Leanne was damned lucky she hadn't been one of them. "Was that before or after Johnny's death?"

"After," Leanne answered after a moment of thought.

If it was right after Johnny's murder, Briar realized, it was possible that Cortland had figured out what Johnny was up to. Had he sent someone to kill Johnny and retrieve what her husband had stolen?

Whoever he'd sent after Johnny clearly hadn't found what he'd been looking for, or Blake and his boys wouldn't be trying to kidnap Logan as leverage to get their hands on what Johnny had stolen.

So where, exactly, had Johnny hidden his bloody secrets?

"How soon after Johnny's death did he stop locking that drawer?" Briar asked.

"I don't remember." Leanne gave Briar a troubled look. "Do you think Johnny took something from Mr. Cortland's office?"

"Do you?"

The other woman looked down at her hands, her brow crinkled with thought. She had neat, well-manicured hands, Briar thought, darting a quick look at her own work-worn hands with their short, uneven nails and the occasional ragged cuticle. Johnny must have looked at this woman and seen everything Briar wasn't.

Maybe she'd been wrong. Maybe their marriage had failed not because Johnny wouldn't grow up but because they'd grown in different directions.

"I wondered if he took something," Leanne said quietly after another moment of silence. "The last time I saw Johnny, he told me I should look for another job. When I asked him why, he said he had a feeling something bad would be going down at the sawmill. He wouldn't tell me what. Wouldn't even tell me why he thought so." She shook her head slowly, tears glistening on the rims of her lower eyelids. "The day of the explosion, I'd taken a day off work to go for a job interview. This job, as a matter of fact."

No wonder Dalton had focused on Leanne Dawson as a person of interest. The coincidence of her being off work that day, and looking for a new job, at that, would have raised his suspicions.

"You were very lucky," Briar said.

"I know. I still can't believe it sometimes. Any of it. Mr. Cortland always seemed so nice and…ordinary."

"That's how it works sometimes." Briar couldn't stop herself from asking one final question. "Do you think Johnny loved you?"

Leanne's sharp blue eyes snapped up to meet Briar's. "That's a strange question from a police officer."

"I know. Forget I asked it."

The other woman's eyes narrowed. "What did you say your name was?"

"Briar Culpepper."

"Oh, my God." Leanne's eyes widened with horror. "You're his wife. Aren't you?"

Briar tried not to react, but her skin was already crawling with regret. She shouldn't have come here and pretended she was just another police officer.

"What, did you want to see what I looked like? See how I compare?" Leanne was crying now, soft silent tears spilling down her cheeks. "Do you want an apology? Because I'll give you one. God knows, I owe it to you."

"I don't want an apology. I believe you when you say you didn't know he was married. I sometimes think Johnny didn't really understand that fact himself." Briar made herself meet the other woman's red-rimmed eyes. "I'm sorry to have come here like this. I'm sorry I wasn't up-front about who I am. But you have to understand—there are people who believe Johnny took something potentially incriminating from Wayne Cortland. Very dangerous people who are willing to go after my son to get that information back."

Leanne's tears kept falling, but her expression shifted from despair to horror. "Someone's gone after your son?"

"Twice, at least. And I don't know what Johnny took, if he took anything at all. Or where he would have hidden it if he did."

"And you think *I* know?"

"I don't know. I was hoping, I guess."

Leanne pulled a box of tissues from her desk drawer and blotted her cheeks. "You're putting a lot more importance on my relationship with Johnny than either he or I did." She took a deep breath and lifted her chin, meeting Briar's gaze. "I knew it was a fling. I knew it was reckless, but he made me feel good, you know? Desirable and maybe a little dangerous myself." Her mouth curved in a self-conscious smile. "I know, me? Dangerous? But that's how he made me feel. Like I could take on the world single-handed. It was an addictive feeling."

Briar's stomach squirmed with sympathy. That had been

Johnny's most potent attraction for her, too, at least when she'd been younger. He'd had the verve and style of a bad boy without really being very dangerous at all. The most harm he'd ever done to anyone was all emotional, and even then, Briar thought, he'd never meant for it to happen.

He hadn't meant to break her heart. Or Leanne Dawson's. And if she was honest, her heart wasn't nearly as affected as her pride.

"You never had any suspicions about Wayne Cortland?" she asked Leanne. "That his business might be a front for something illegal?"

"Of course not. I wouldn't have worked for him if I had."

She sounded honest, Briar thought. There was nothing in her tone to even hint at deception. Wayne Cortland had played the part of the honest businessman very, very well. It was why he'd gotten away with his crimes so long in the first place.

"Thank you for your time, Ms. Dawson. I appreciate it. And again, I'm sorry for not telling you who I was up front."

Leanne shook her head. "I'm sorry I couldn't be more help."

Briar had gotten halfway to the doorway when she heard footsteps coming up behind her in a rush. She turned on her heel so quickly that Leanne nearly rammed into her headfirst.

The other woman took a quick step back, wobbling for balance. "Sorry," she said. "I just thought of something. I don't know if it means anything to you—it didn't to me. But that day Johnny told me to look for another job, I'd made a joke about stocking my pantry while I could in case the winter turned out to be a lean one. And he said he never had to worry about stocking his pantry. He had so much stored away folks were starting to think he was a doomsday prepper."

Briar released a soft huff of laughter. "If he'd had to stock things away for himself, he'd have starved."

"I never thought him one for gardening," Leanne admitted. "I was just sitting here thinking about that conversation and it struck me you must have been the one who stocked that pantry he was talking about."

Briar nodded. "Is that the strange thing you remembered?"

"No, it's what he said after that. He said, 'It's amazing how many different things you can store in a Mason jar.' And then he winked at me and headed off on his truck route."

Briar felt a little tremor run up her spine.

"Do you think that means anything?" Leanne asked.

Briar kept her expression neutral. "I doubt it. He's right—there are all kinds of things you can put away in a Mason jar. He was probably just trying to sound naughty and secretive."

Leanne's curious expression shifted to a mixture of fondness and regret. "That was Johnny, all right." Her face reddened. "I'm sorry. I guess you'd know that a lot better than I did."

"Do me a favor, Leanne, okay? Stop beating yourself up about Johnny. The only thing you did wrong was fall for his lines. You weren't the first girl to do that, you know."

"Thank you. And I hope you find what you're looking for and that everything goes well for you and your son."

Briar smiled again and turned back toward the door, trying not to let her suddenly energized legs break into a run as she headed out into the waning daylight.

It was after four when she pulled her Jeep out of the Pinter Construction parking lot. The drive back to Bitterwood would take more than three hours, an interminable amount of time when she was now almost certain where she'd find whatever it was that Johnny had stolen from Wayne Cortland.

It couldn't have been files, at least not the paper-and-ink sort of files, because there wasn't a Mason jar in her stash at home big enough to contain that sort of contraband. But maybe Johnny had taken photos of the files and stored them on a memory chip. Or even a flash drive. Either of those things would be small enough to store inside a jar of peach preserves or pickled okra. Store it inside a pill bottle or a small film canister, wrap it in a zippered plastic bag and shove it into a jar of canned vegetables or fruit, and almost nobody would think to look for it there. The plastic would protect it from the canned food, and the food would protect it from easy detection.

The only danger would have been if Briar had pulled that particular jar from the shelf and opened it. And since she had a particular system of storing things, oldest in front, newest in back, Johnny could easily have chosen the least likely jar to be opened right away.

All she had to do was go through the jars that would have been at the back of her stash at the time of Johnny's death and see which one held his secret.

Her phone trilled as she pulled out into traffic on the four-lane that led to the interstate highway, but when she tried to answer, she got a "low battery" message. "Damn it." She couldn't even see who had called.

There was a charger in the glove compartment. At the next traffic light, she pulled out the charger, hooked it to the cigarette lighter and plugged in her phone. The display came on and she saw that the missed call had been from Dana Massey. She called her back.

Dana answered on the first ring. "Briar? Where are you?"

"In Wytheville, Virginia," she answered. "Long story. What's up?"

"I've been trying to call Dalton for the last hour, and nobody's answering. Is he with you?"

Alarm rattled her nerves. "No. He should be at home. He's watching Logan for me."

Dana's silence raised her panic level by several notches.

"Maybe he's not answering any calls but mine," Briar ventured.

"That could be it." Dana sounded relieved by the thought. "Why don't you call him and see what's up? And then tell him to give me a call. I may have some information for him about a group of anarchists he's been trying to tie to Blake Culpepper. But I've been given the okay to talk only to Dalton."

"I'll tell him." She hung up and tried Dalton's cell phone. After five rings the phone went to voice mail. She left a message, then tried his home number.

She got a busy signal.

Maybe he didn't have call waiting, she told herself as she set the phone on the seat to continue charging.

But twenty minutes later when she tried the house phone again, she got another busy signal.

After a third try, she called Dana back. "There's something wrong," she told Dalton's sister. "And I'm three hours away."

"I'm still in Knoxville, but I'll call Nix and have him check on Dalton and Logan. I'll get there as soon as I can." Dana hung up the phone without saying goodbye.

Briar set the phone on the passenger seat, her heart starting to race as she pushed the Jeep's speed as high as she dared.

Chapter Thirteen

Someone was hammering outside the house. The sound droned on and on, setting off painful throbs in the middle of Dalton's forehead. He struggled to open his eyes, trying to stand up and cross to the door to yell at the offender to stop with all the noise.

But his eyelids seemed as heavy as boulders, and the hint of daylight that crept between the narrow openings felt like stiletto knives being rammed into his eyeballs. Nausea rolled through his gut in greasy waves, forcing him to be very still. For a second the hammering went silent, so silent that he feared for a moment that he'd been struck instantly deaf.

Then it started again, louder and more urgent than before.

Not hammering, he realized. Knocking.

Someone was knocking on his door.

He tried to sit up, but the world spun wildly around him, and he couldn't stop the nausea that time. The best he could do was direct his sickness away from the sofa onto the floor below.

"Dalton, it's Doyle. Are you in there?"

He couldn't move, except the helpless heaving that finished emptying his stomach onto the floor. What the hell was wrong with him?

He was home. He could tell that much from the smell of the place, the feel of the nubby sofa fabric against his cheek, the bits and pieces of decor he could see through the narrow slits of his eyelids. He tried to answer Doyle, but his aching throat felt dust dry.

A minute later he heard the door open. The sound of footsteps rushed toward him, stuttering to a stop a few feet away.

"Dalton!" Doyle said sharply.

Dalton managed a groan. He felt hands on his face. Warm, rough hands.

"Can you breathe?"

I am breathing, he thought, but he realized he wasn't. He concentrated on taking a breath, then another.

His head felt heavy and thick, but the air moving in and out of his lungs had a clarifying effect. Some of the dizzying pain in his head subsided, and the next time he tried to open his eyes, he was able to do it with minimal effort. "I don't feel good."

"I can see that." Doyle touched his fingertips to Dalton's throat. Checking his pulse, Dalton realized.

"What happened to me?" he asked.

"You tell me. What do you remember?"

Nothing, Dalton realized with a rush of panic. He remembered going to bed the night before and then...

Nothing.

"Where's Logan?" Doyle asked.

Dalton stared at his brother. "I don't know. Oh, God." He tried to get up from the sofa but the movement made his head spin again. He swallowed the nausea and tried to push up again.

"Sit still. I'll check." Doyle pulled his phone out of his pocket and headed out of the room. Going to search the downstairs, Dalton realized after a moment of confusion. Being thorough.

He stared down at the vomit on the floor. Not a lot, he saw. Mostly liquid. Had he eaten breakfast? He looked at his watch. Almost five. Morning or afternoon?

Afternoon, he decided, noting the western light. He'd lost nearly a whole day.

"Where's Briar?" he asked as Doyle came back through the living room, heading for the stairs.

"She's on her way back from Wytheville." Doyle paused on the stairs. "You don't remember her leaving?"

"I don't remember today," he answered, trying to stand up again. "I don't remember anything since going to bed last night. At least, I think it was last night."

The look Doyle shot his way scared the hell out of him. But his brother started back up the stairs quickly, not commenting.

He needed to clean up the mess on the floor, Dalton thought. He didn't want Logan or Briar to see the mess.

Staggering to the kitchen to grab a roll of paper towels, he returned to the sofa and tried to lever himself down far enough to mop up the mess. But even bending over made his head spin.

He did what he could, cleaning between bouts of dizziness. Finally, though the floor would need a good mopping, at least he was no longer staring down at his own stomach contents.

Doyle came down the stairs slowly, his expression grim. His gaze met Dalton's briefly, then skittered away. He pulled out his phone and made another call. "I need everyone available to meet me at Hale's place. 224 Maplewood Lane in Edgewood. We need to put out an Amber Alert. Logan Blackwood is missing."

Dalton felt sick all over again.

HE'S JUST HIDING. He's hiding, and when he hears my voice, he'll come out and everything will be okay.

Except Briar knew it wasn't true. Too much time had passed.

The call from Dana Massey had come somewhere around Bristol, Tennessee, while Briar was still more than two hours out of Bitterwood. The rest of the drive home had been a blur, driven at speeds that risked pursuit by the Tennessee Highway Patrol. She'd traded calls with Dana, Nix and even the chief himself during the drive, all apprising her of the latest information.

But no call from Dalton. Dalton, whom she'd trusted to protect her child while she was away.

Nobody had said much about Dalton.

The guard at the gatehouse had looked grim as he let her through into the subdivision. Flashing blue-and-red lights cut through the evening gloom, each swirling pulse a grim beacon, drawing her into her worst nightmare.

Nix stood sentry on the porch. He met her halfway up the walk, his hands closing over her arms. "We're going to get him back."

"I know that," she said shortly. "Where's Dalton?"

"Inside." The corners of Nix's mouth tightened.

"What aren't y'all telling me?" she asked as she walked with him up the porch steps.

He caught her hand in his, turning her to face him when they reached the door. "You know I'd be happy to blame him for everything, but we're pretty sure he was drugged somehow."

She looked up at him through narrowed eyes. "Drugged?"

"Paramedics came to look him over. He's coming down off whatever it was, but he has all the symptoms of some sort of drug ingestion. They got a blood sample to test.

They wanted to take him to the hospital, but he wouldn't budge until you got here."

The ache in the center of Briar's gut intensified. "What did he say happened?"

"That's just it. He doesn't remember." Nix's grip on her arm eased into a gentle caress. "Hopefully the test will tell us more, but given the memory loss and his other symptoms, I'm guessing it was something like GHB or Rohypnol."

Both date-rape drugs, Briar thought. GHB—gamma hydroxybutyrate—might be more likely, especially if her cousin Blake was behind what had happened. GHB could be cooked easily enough, and the Blue Ridge Infantry was all tangled up with mountain meth mechanics these days. "How did someone get close enough to drug him?"

"That's what we're trying to figure out. The TBI has been here an hour, going over the place with tweezers. If there's a clue to be found, they'll find it," Nix assured her.

"What about the gatekeeper?" she asked. "Nobody gets in or out of this subdivision without passing through the gate."

"We're trying to find the daytime guard. He went off duty around five—he was gone before we figured out we needed to talk to him, and nobody seems to know where he went. His replacement said he mentioned something about doing some nighttime crappie fishing. We're trying to track down where that might be, but he's not answering his cell phone."

"Do you think he could be in danger?"

"I don't know. Probably not."

"I need to talk to Dalton."

Nix squeezed her hand. "You're not going to be able to make him feel any worse than he already does."

She didn't want to make him feel worse, she realized. As

much as she was aching inside, aching like a bad tooth, she couldn't find it in her to vent that pain, or the rising anger filling her gut, on Dalton. She'd nearly lost her son right out of her own arms once, hadn't she? If Dalton hadn't intervened that night at the cabin, she didn't think she could have stopped those men from taking her son.

And one look at Dalton, sitting on his sofa with his head in his hands, was enough to drive away even the thought of blame.

He looked up at the sound of her footsteps, his face a road map of guilt and grief. "I'm so sorry."

She sat beside him, wrapping her arms around him. "Are you okay?"

He shrugged away from her grasp. "Don't, Briar."

She dropped her hands to her lap. "You can't remember anything?"

"I remember…last night."

She thought about the night before, how she'd sat on this very couch, anchoring Dalton's hips between her thighs as they'd strained toward some ephemeral promise of release. Just two people seeking pleasure in each other—as natural as breathing.

Profanely distant from this horrible moment some twenty-four hours later, she thought. "You don't remember waking me this morning to tell me you had to go see your father in the hospital?"

His gaze snapped up to meet hers. "My father's in the hospital?"

She could see the shock and fear in his eyes, as immediate and real as it had been early this morning when he'd awakened her to tell her he was on his way to the hospital.

"He's okay," she said quickly. "Just a panic attack. They transferred him back to the jail around lunchtime."

He looked as if she'd just punched him. "I don't remember."

"Nix says you were probably drugged."

He shook his head, stopping quickly. His face turned a sickly shade of gray, and for a moment Briar thought he was going to be sick. Color seeped back into his face after a moment. "I wouldn't have let anyone in. How could I be drugged?"

"Maybe they forced their way in?" she suggested, but even as the words left her mouth, she could see that while the room showed signs of having undergone a search by the crime scene unit, it showed no signs of a struggle.

"I don't think so," Dalton murmured. "They said I must have ingested whatever it was. That's how those kinds of drugs are usually administered."

"I guess the question now is, who would you have trusted to let into your house while Logan was here?"

He leaned back, resting his head on the sofa cushion behind him. "I've been wondering the same thing. It couldn't have been just anyone. I wouldn't have let just anyone in."

"Then think about it. Who would you trust enough?"

"My mother," he said immediately. "But there's no way she's involved."

"Okay. Who else?"

He rubbed his jaw, looking sick again. "Tom Bevill," he said. His boss at the county prosecutor's office. "Laney. Any Bitterwood cop, I guess."

That might be a problem, she thought, since they weren't yet certain that everyone on the force could be trusted. "Anyone else?"

He looked at her again. "Most of the attorneys at the office, if they were bringing files from work for some reason. My secretary. Maybe some of the clerks."

"What about Lydia?" she asked, thinking of the blonde she'd met in his office.

"No, not Lydia." He swallowed hard, his Adam's apple bobbing. "They still can't find George Applewood? The security guard at the gate?"

"He went fishing, they think. He's not answering his phone." At least, she hoped that was the situation. If he'd seen who'd come through that gate, he might be a witness.

And the people they were dealing with right now didn't seem the sort who'd care to leave witnesses.

"What are we going to do, Briar? What have I done?"

She rose from the sofa and sat on the coffee table in front of him, catching his face between her hands. A day's growth of beard scraped her palms as she forced him to look at her.

"I'm going to find Logan. That's what I'm going to do. And when I do, I'm gonna make whoever took him regret the sorry day they came mewlin' and squirmin' into this world."

Dalton's eyes were red-veined, his pupils a little dilated, but he found it within himself to meet and hold her gaze. "Don't leave me out of this, Briar. Please don't cut me off."

She dropped her hands to his shoulder. "You're in no condition to go lookin' for kidnappers in the mountains. You can't even see straight."

"So give me something. There's got to be a way to counteract this thing, right? Call the paramedics back here—they'll know what to do."

"I'm sure they already gave you something if there was something that could be done."

His brow furrowed, as if he were trying to remember.

"They said it's possible he vomited up a fair bit of the dose." Dana Massey had walked up behind her. She came around the coffee table and sat beside Dalton. "They tried to get him to go to the hospital for further treatment, but he refused to go."

"I had to talk to you first," Dalton told Briar. "I needed to tell you how sorry I am."

She put her hand on his knee. "You need time to let the rest of the drug get out of your system."

"We don't have time."

"Dalton—" Briar looked at Dana for support.

But Dana returned her look with hard determination. "He needs to be part of this. He's a lot more lucid than he was when I got here."

"Has anyone contacted you?" Dalton asked, making a visible effort to pull himself together.

"No," she answered, wondering why she hadn't even thought about getting a call from the kidnappers. That was the point of taking Logan from her, wasn't it? To get her to turn over whatever Johnny had taken.

At least now she had a pretty good idea where to look for his secrets.

She hadn't told the others, she realized. Why hadn't she? *Because they might try to stop you.*

She was a police officer. She knew as well as anyone how the police would want to handle it. Stall for time to make a copy of whatever Johnny had stolen, assuming it was Wayne Cortland's secret books. Leave Logan in the grasp of men who were more than willing to risk his life for their own purposes. All in pursuit of a "greater good." As if there was a greater good than getting her son back.

Would Dalton feel the same way?

She studied his face, took in the shadows of fear in his eyes and the lines of desperation carving deep valleys in his handsome features. She wanted desperately to believe she could trust him.

But right now she didn't trust anyone. Not even Nix.

She barely even trusted herself.

To hell with letting the police call the shots this time. Her son was with people who had no trouble killing innocents. She'd seen what they'd done to Tommy Barnett. And a little boy like Logan would be so easy to harm, even if it wasn't their intention....

"I need to be alone." Her mind had already moved several steps ahead toward what needed to be done next. Now, before anyone tried to contact her. Before the clock truly started ticking.

Dalton's gaze narrowed. Just a tiny twitch, but she had come to know him well enough in the last couple of days to know what it meant.

He wondered what she was up to.

Digging deep, she found the core of steel it took to lie to his face. "I just need to be away from you for a little while."

He flinched almost as surely as if she'd slapped him with her hand instead of her words.

"Briar—" Dana looked shocked.

"My son is missing." Briar pushed to her feet, letting her voice rise with pent-up anguish. "I think that earns me the right to feel a little anger!"

She saw Doyle and Nix both turn their heads to look at her.

Now, she thought. *I have to move now.*

She strode toward the door, her jaw set with determination. If they tried to stop her, she'd make them get out of her way.

But Nix and Doyle stepped back, giving her unhindered access to the door. When Dana came up quickly behind her, Nix shook his head.

Dalton's voice rose from his place on the sofa. "Let her go. Give her what she needs."

The grief in his voice burned like fire in her ears, but she didn't let it stop her from walking out the door.

Outside, night had fallen completely, deepened by rain clouds scudding eastward toward the mountains. There would be no moon out tonight, she thought with satisfaction.

That was good. The darkness would make her approach to the cabin that much harder to detect.

They would be watching for her. She was certain of it. They must know by now she knew her son was missing. That she'd know who had taken him and why.

Maybe that's why they were waiting to contact her. Why risk it when all they had to do was wait at her cabin for her to make her move? They could swoop in, overpower her, and take what they wanted. No mess. No real risk.

But there was something she knew about the cabin that they didn't. Something nobody outside her family had known. Not even Johnny.

She knew a way to get into the cabin without being seen.

Chapter Fourteen

All the air seemed to rush from the room when Briar walked out. Dalton pushed up from the sofa and waited for another dizzy spell to hit, but it didn't materialize. He moved away from the door into the kitchen and stood there for a moment, looking around. Trying to remember.

There was a bowl on the table. The remains of chicken noodle soup. *Logan,* he thought, pain ripping through him like shrapnel. Had the boy been right here with him when someone had come to see him?

Why had he let anyone in? What had he been thinking?

He needed to get out of here. He needed to go out there and start looking for Logan. He didn't know where to start, but he couldn't just sit here and pretend that sweet child wasn't out there somewhere in desperate danger.

And if he couldn't do it, he realized, his gut knotting with a fresh new wave of anxiety, neither could Briar.

She hadn't left to get away from him. At least, that hadn't been her only reason.

"Briar's going to go off alone if we let her," he warned Dana as she walked up beside him and put her hand on his shoulder.

Dana looked at him in alarm. "You think she's going after Culpepper?"

"I don't know. I just know it's not like Briar to need

time alone. She'd stay here and say what she thought. She left because she wants to get away from here without anybody questioning her."

Dana looked across the room to where Doyle and Nix were talking quietly near the door. "They're not going to just let you walk out of here."

"There's a back door," he murmured.

"You can barely stand."

"I'm good. I'm feeling clearheaded now."

"You can't drive."

"You can."

She stared at him. "You want me to sneak you out of here? Lie to my brother and the man I love so you can wander off, drug-addled, after Briar?"

"If she goes alone, she could be in serious trouble."

"We tell Nix and Doyle or it doesn't happen," she said flatly.

Dalton grimaced. Neither man would be willing to let him go after Briar. Not without a long, time-eating argument.

"Okay, fine. We'll tell them. Convince them how important it is for us to go after her. Just let me go to the bathroom first and I'll come back. We'll tell them together."

He headed for the bathroom down a short hallway off the living room. But he bypassed that door and went straight out to the garage instead.

Going through the garage door would be faster, but the sound of the big door opening would bring Dana and the others running before he could get away. Instead, he grabbed the spare car key from the tool drawer where he kept it and went through the side door, hurrying around the garage.

To his surprise, Briar's Jeep was still parked in the driveway next to his car. She sat in the driver's seat, her head low, her white-knuckled hands gripping the steering wheel as if it were a lifeline.

He knocked on the passenger window, making her jump. Her gray eyes widened at the sight of him.

"I know you're going to go find Logan. Let me go with you," he said through the glass.

She continued looking at him, unblinking, for so long he almost forgot to breathe again. Then she reached over and unlocked the door.

He pulled himself into the passenger seat and turned to look at her. "I thought you'd already be gone."

"I thought I would be, too," she admitted.

"There are so many things I want to say to you. How sorry I am that I failed you and Logan. But in a minute Dana's going to realize I've been in the bathroom too long. A few minutes after that, they'll come looking for us. So if we're going, we need to go now."

She gazed solemnly at him for a few seconds longer, then put the Jeep in Neutral. The vehicle began to roll quietly backward down the gently sloping driveway. Wrestling with the wheel, she turned the Jeep onto the street and started the engine.

Dalton glanced back at the house. So far the front door remained closed. But it wouldn't stay that way for long. "They'll be coming after us."

"I know. I just need to get there first."

"To the cabin?" he asked.

"Yes. Although I should warn you—they'll have it staked out."

"The police? Or the kidnappers?"

"The kidnappers." She glanced at the rearview mirror and pulled suddenly down a side road.

"But we're going there? Just the two of us?" He grabbed the seat belt and wrapped it around him, even as she took another curve at a scary rate of speed, threatening to send him sliding into the floorboard. His stomach roiled at the thought of walking into an ambush. He was still feeling a little woozy, as much as he didn't want to admit it. Hardly in any condition to fight his way out of a mess.

"I think I know where Johnny hid what he stole from Cortland."

Dalton stopped in the middle of buckling the belt. "You know what he took? Was it Cortland's cooked books?"

"I didn't say I knew what he took. Only that I think I know where he hid it." She told him about her conversation with Leanne Dawson.

"He hid something in a jar of preserves?"

"Or pickles or stewed tomatoes. Something like that."

"Can't be physical files," Dalton said, trying to hide his sense of deflation.

"Could be photographs of files stored on a flash drive or a memory card," Briar said, making him feel like an idiot.

Of course, she was right. In fact, it made much more sense that Johnny Blackwood might make some sort of copy than try to steal the files themselves. If he'd taken the books, they'd have been missed. "Wouldn't putting them into something like preserves risk ruining the storage disk? I mean, I know he'd have stored them in something airtight, but—"

"I don't think he considered it to be a place of long-term storage," she said, whipping around another corner. He finished buckling his seat belt quickly, bracing his feet on the floorboard to keep from sliding into her. "I'm obsessive about using my canned goods by a certain date. So I know they haven't had a chance to go bad on us. He'd have put the disk in one of the newer jars, since I'd use them last. But he knew how I did things. He knew that if something happened, I'd open the jar within a year. Either to eat what was stored inside or to dispose of it."

"But what if you threw away the jar unopened?"

She shot him a look. "You don't throw away a jar. You sterilize it and use it again."

"Ah." He was beginning to understand the brilliance of using Briar's food stores as a hiding place. The average person wouldn't think to look inside a jar of pickles for a computer storage disk. But Briar would open the jar sooner or later because she wasn't the sort to waste anything. Resourceful woman, his Briar.

My Briar, he reiterated silently, a strange thrill running through his body like a jolt of electricity.

Mine.

"He probably thought he could keep rehiding the thing as long as he needed to," she said as they pulled onto Cherokee Road. "Of course, he didn't know I was planning to divorce him."

"So if the kidnappers have the cabin staked out, how are we going to get inside it to look for the file?"

Her lips curved upward at the corners. Not quite a smile, but it gave him hope to see something besides harsh lines of fear and anger on Briar's face. "You'll see."

DURING PROHIBITION in the 1920s and 1930s, liquor sales hadn't ended in the mountains any more than they had anywhere else in the country. They'd simply gone underground. Instead of the speakeasies and organized-crime control of liquor production and sales found in the bigger cities, bootleggers and moonshine stills had ruled the day in the mountains, even after the Twenty-First Amendment had ended Prohibition in the United States. After all, many of Tennessee's counties were still dry counties.

And people still liked to get hammered now and then.

For Briar's maternal great-grandfather, distilling moon-shine had paid his bills and fed his kids long after 1933, when the rest of the country went back to drinking as usual. But the revenuers could be ruthless in their quest to shut down any distillery not putting money into the government coffers, so old Bartholomew Meade had come up with his own way of protecting his home-brew business from government scrutiny.

He'd learned, literally by accident, that his cabin was built very close to an underground cavern. His eldest son, Lamar, had fallen through an opening in the cave while hunting for rabbits in the woods about fifty yards from home. Unable to climb back up the hole, he'd followed the narrow cave to its exit deep in the mountains. When Bart Meade had realized he had a natural tunnel not fifty yards from his house, he saw the advantage it would give him over other moonshiners, who had to risk carrying their contraband over ground.

It had taken nearly two years of backbreaking labor for Bart and his three sons and two daughters to dig a tunnel between the root cellar beneath his cabin and the natural cave fifty yards away, but they'd done it, and the Meade family had thrived on their law-defying industry for several decades to come, until the 1960s, when Bitterwood had voted to allow the sale of liquor in hopes of drawing in tourists headed for the national park.

The still had been long gone by the time Briar's mother had deeded the cabin to her as a sort of dowry. But the tunnel was still there, mostly unused but still in good shape. And still a secret known only to descendants of Bartholomew Meade. Not even Johnny had known about the tunnel. Briar had never even thought to tell him about it.

Strange that she felt no qualms in telling Dalton about it now.

"It's called Smuggler's Cave by the Cherokee Cove locals," she told him as they made their way up the mountain toward the cave entrance. "My great-granddaddy made sure all the locals heard lurid tales about how the place was haunted. Fear of haints kept all but the most intrepid away. And the ones who didn't fall for the legend of Smuggler's Cave found themselves picking buckshot out of their backsides if they got too close to the place." She flashed him a wry grin.

"So your great-granddaddy was a moonshiner?" he asked as he followed her up the side of the mountain toward the cave entrance. A storm was brewing, lightning snapping and crackling on the western horizon. Clouds had begun to obscure the moon, making the last quarter mile of their trek up the mountain more difficult than Briar had hoped.

At least the hours that it had taken her to drive back from Virginia had helped dilute the effects of whatever drug Dalton had ingested. He was keeping up with her surprisingly well as they climbed the steep hillside.

"Technically," she reminded him, "yours was, too. On Tallie Cumberland's side. The Meades and the Cumberlands were bootlegging rivals back in the day."

"But wouldn't Blake know about this secret passageway already, since he's your cousin?"

"He's a cousin on my daddy's side. The Meades were my mama's people. Culpeppers and Meades were nearly as bitter rivals as the Meades and Cumberlands."

"Ah, a Romeo and Juliet story."

"Well, except my parents weren't fool enough to kill themselves over it," she said flatly. "Lucky for me."

It was strange to hear her own voice so calm and uninflected, considering the violent storm of terror ripping around inside her gut. The thought of Logan being held even for a moment in the rough and ruthless custody of her cousin Blake and his band of cutthroats had damned near paralyzed her earlier as she sat in her Jeep trying to figure out what to do next. If Dalton hadn't knocked on her window…

As if he sensed the turn of her thoughts, Dalton touched her arm as they neared the mouth of the cavern. "Briar, we're going to find Logan. I won't stop until we do."

She looked up at him. He was barely visible in the gloom, but the fierce determination in his eyes was impossible to miss, even in the dark. "I don't know what's going to happen once we get to the root cellar. They may have people already positioned inside the cabin. We could walk straight into an ambush."

"They're not going to hurt you as long as they think you can give them those files."

"I don't know why it hasn't occurred to them that I could have already made a dozen copies."

"I've been thinking about that," Dalton told her as he followed her through the dark mouth of the cavern. What little ambient light had illuminated their path outside disappeared, the darkness swallowing them completely.

Briar went still, just listening for a moment. She felt Dalton at her back, the heat of his body close and comforting. Quelling the urge to lean back into his solid warmth, she turned on the small flashlight she'd brought with her from the Jeep.

Damp stone walls continued for several yards ahead before twisting out of sight. She realized with a sudden flutter of alarm that she hadn't been in this tunnel for over a year. There could have been a cave-in she didn't know about. But the tunnel had remained solid and unshakable for decades. She had no reason to think it would fail on her now, did she? God knew, her day had already seen sufficient trouble without borrowing any more.

"You've been thinking about what?" she asked a moment later, when she was satisfied no pressing danger lurked ahead of them in the cavern tunnel.

"About why they don't care if we make a copy."

She looked back at him, shining the flashlight toward his face so she could read his expression. He squinted but didn't look away. "Why don't they care?" she asked.

"Because they don't have the information themselves. Cortland died in the blast. Merritt Cortland is almost certainly dead himself, whether we can find his body or not. I'm betting those two may have been the only people in the whole organization who knew all the connections. Blake Culpepper doesn't give a damn whether or not the police scoop up the people Cortland had working for him. He'd probably thank us for it."

"But he needs to know who they are. Who might turn state's evidence," Briar realized, following his thoughts. "Who to eliminate as a rival."

"It's a crash course in mountain crime," Dalton said. "If we want to understand how Cortland ran his crew, we need to get our hands on his files. Blake and I both want the same thing. For very different reasons."

Briar swung the flashlight toward the tunnel. "Then let's see what we can do to make that happen."

"I DON'T THINK we should drive right up to Briar's place," Walker Nix warned his boss as they neared the turnoff on the mountain road. Beside him, Dana's hands were clenched tight in her lap, her jaw as rigid as stone. Dalton had ditched her, and she was still smarting a little from the betrayal, even though she and her brother had both admitted, in response to Nix's confession, that like Nix, they'd probably have done the same thing if they'd been in Dalton's position.

"You think there are bears in the woods?" Doyle asked drily, slowing the truck's speed in response to Nix's warning. Nix knew he wasn't talking about real bears.

"It's what I'd do if I were Blake Culpepper. I've got her kid. Now she's going to make her move and find what she's going to have to give me if she wants Logan back. Everything in the world points to the answer being in Briar's cabin, but so far nobody's been able to find it."

"Do you think Briar's known what it is and where to find it all along?" Dana asked quietly.

"Not all along, no. But given the fact that she bailed on us, I think maybe she figured it out sometime today. I think she knows where to look, and she's not going to let us stop her from handing it over if she finds it."

"She's just going to hand over evidence to a criminal?"

Nix looked over Dana's head at her brother. "If I had to guess, she'd like to let things play out without having to give Blake anything he's asking for, but if it comes to a choice between the law and her son—"

"Of course she'll choose her son," Dana said flatly. "I'm pretty sure any one of us would do the same. *Will* do the same."

Nix couldn't argue with that statement. Apparently, neither could the chief. He went on past the turnoff, slanting a look toward Nix. "What now?"

"We park down the road and go on foot. Carefully."

THE CAVE CAME to an abrupt end, the twisting footpath running out at a solid stone wall. At least, Dalton thought it was solid until Briar pressed her fingers into a small rocky indentation on the left side of the wall and a dark seam appeared in the stone face.

It was a door, he saw, set into the rock by someone highly skilled and, apparently, deeply secretive. It swung open into the cave, revealing little more than darkness beyond.

Briar flicked on her flashlight, illuminating the dark space in front of them. Metal shelves tightly packed with jars of preserved food stood about two feet in front of the door, reflecting the flashlight beam back to them. "My stores," she whispered shortly, slipping into the tight space between the doorway and the shelves.

Dalton followed her down the narrow corridor between the shelves and the wall until they emerged in the center of a small densely packed cellar lined with the metal shelves of Mason jars on one side and large root bins on the other. Briar flipped a light switch and a bare bulb gave off a muted glow overhead, revealing more of the cellar.

To Dalton's left, a set of concrete block steps led up to a flat door that opened upward rather than out. "Where does that door go?"

"The side yard." Briar pointed out another, normal door at the top of a set of wooden stairs. "That door leads up to the house."

Dalton nodded toward the rows of Mason jars. "Is this where you think Johnny hid whatever he took from Cortland?"

She nodded. "I just have to figure out which jar."

"His last day driving the Travisville route for Davenport Trucking was August 15 of last year."

She nodded. "He died on the eighteenth. So it would have had to be in something I put away before the eighteenth but probably no further back than, say, June of last year." She looked at the jars. "Peach preserves, apples, pickles, peppers, squash, tomatoes—all summer crops.

Too late for strawberries, too early for the winter squashes and pears."

He looked at the rows of jars, feeling overwhelmed. "We have to open all of them?"

"Well, the most likely options would be the preserves. Most of the others are stored in brine or clear juice, but the preserves would be opaque. Better for hiding something." She crossed to a section of the shelves lined with jars of bright golden peach preserves. Dalton followed her, looking over her shoulder as she pointed to the label. "Here's the canning date. Look for anything between July and August 18 of last year."

He started culling jars with those dates. "Should we open them all?"

She looked up at him, frowning. "I realize this is going to sound strange from a woman who's terrified for the safety of her son, but these are his favorites, and I'd rather not ruin them if we can figure out which one is the right one." She turned the jar she held on its side and gave it a little shake. She set it to one side and started to do the same thing to the next jar in her stack. Dalton followed suit, trying to figure out if there was something besides peaches in each of the jars.

"Oh," Briar said a few minutes later, drawing Dalton's gaze. She was holding a jar up toward the overhead bulb. Pressing against the side of the jar, Dalton saw with a flutter of excitement, was the corner of a plastic bag.

Briar twisted off the band that held the vacuum-sealed lid on the jar. Pulling a small knife from her jeans pocket, she pried up the lid until it released with a soft pop. "Grab that bucket in the corner," she told Dalton. He brought it to her and she slowly poured out the sticky fruit contents of the jar until a small zip-sealed sandwich bag fell into the bucket.

She plucked it out with her thumb and forefinger, using the knife blade to scrape off as much of the peach preserves as she could.

Inside, wrapped in more clear plastic, was a small black flash drive.

Chapter Fifteen

Dalton didn't know what he'd expected Briar to do when she found Johnny's hidden secret, but dissolving into tears wasn't it. Big gulping sobs seemed to burst from her throat, beyond her ability to control, as she clutched the sticky bag to her chest and shook with tears. "I was so afraid," she said. "So afraid it wouldn't be here. I didn't know what I was going to do if it wasn't here."

He crossed to her side and put his arms around her, half expecting her to push him away. But she let him hold her, pressing her forehead against his shoulder and wetting his shirt with her tears. "I'm sorry," she said, her voice raw with emotion. "I'm sorry."

She'd been holding herself together by sheer will, he realized, despite her earlier show of composure. Pressing a kiss to her hair, he murmured soft words of comfort, not inclined to hurry her through this reaction to the stress and fear she'd been laboring under since Doyle had called her to break the news about Logan's disappearance.

But she finally gave herself a shake and pushed her damp curls away from her tearstained face, flashing him a wobbly smile. "That must have been a sight."

"I've felt like doing the same thing for the last three hours," he admitted. "I'm so sorry about losing Logan."

"Someone drugged you."

"Someone I let into my house," he said bluntly. "Why would I do such a thing with Logan in danger?" The question haunted him, not least because he could remember nothing. Not a hint of anything that had happened to him between bedtime the night before and waking on the sofa to Doyle's knock on the door.

"We'll figure it out later," she said firmly, closing her hands over his arms and giving him a little shake. "For now, we need to figure out what to do with this flash drive."

"I wonder why Blake hasn't already called you to make a trade."

She looked down at the sticky plastic bag, grimacing at the mess the preserves had made on the front of her jacket. "I'm not sure how Blake even knows this thing exists, unless Johnny told someone about it."

"Whom might he have told?"

"Nobody in his family. He didn't have much to do with his kin. I guess maybe somebody at the trucking company, maybe one of the other drivers."

Dalton frowned, trying to remember what he'd learned about Johnny's job at Davenport Trucking. "What if he mentioned something to Paul Bailey?"

Briar looked up at him. "If he did, no wonder he ended up dead. Bailey was completely in Wayne Cortland's pocket. But wouldn't Johnny have known that, if he was copying the files?"

"Maybe he tried warning someone else at Davenport about what Bailey was up to. Maybe someone he didn't know he couldn't trust, either."

Briar walked the plastic bag across the cramped little cellar to an ancient sink standing against one wall. She pulled a paper towel from the holder that hung above the sink and wet it with water from the tap, then went about scrubbing off the remainder of the preserves clinging to the plastic bag. "Johnny never did know who to trust."

"He should have told you. If this was really about stopping Cortland." He didn't want to ask the next question, but he forced the words from his mouth anyway. "Do you think he wanted to stop Cortland? Or was this about getting the information for his own purposes?"

She looked up sharply. "You mean blackmail?"

"That. Or even to set up his own network."

One corner of her mouth curved upward. "Definitely not that. Johnny wasn't that ambitious. I don't really see him as a blackmailer, either."

"So maybe he really did want to stop what Cortland was doing?"

"Maybe." She didn't sound very convinced of that option, either, he noticed. No matter what else he'd been, Johnny Blackwood had clearly been an idiot. He'd had Briar and Logan, and he'd been on the verge of throwing it all away because of his lies and infidelity.

If Dalton had been in his shoes...

You'd have done what, hotshot? Let some stranger into your house to pump you full of drugs and take the kid right out from under your nose?

"Johnny's old computer is upstairs in the bedroom." Briar's voice dragged him from an abyss of self-indictment. "I haven't turned it on in months, but it probably still works. Want to take a look at what's on the disk?"

THE POLICE HAD taken Johnny's computer not long after his death, hoping to discover some clue to the motive behind his murder. They'd returned it after the fruitless search, and Briar had put it on a table in her bedroom and mostly ignored it except to dust around it now and then.

She held her breath waiting for the system to boot up,

feeling the seconds ticking inexorably away from her. Why hadn't Blake made his move? What if Logan's kidnapping had nothing to do with this flash drive at all? What then?

Dalton's hand flattened against her back between her shoulder blades, as if he'd sensed she needed his grounding touch to keep herself from going off the rails. "Just breathe," he murmured.

The welcome screen popped up, and for an anxious moment Briar couldn't remember Johnny's password. Fingers fumbling on the keyboard, she typed in a couple of possible passwords before she remembered what had been important to her late husband. *PontiacFirebird92* got her into the system.

"Interesting password," Dalton said.

"Men and their cars," she said shortly, not wanting to dwell on the memories. One of the first things she'd had to do after Johnny's death was sell his beloved Firebird to pay off Johnny's debts and put a little savings away for the coming lean times. Going from two incomes to one, with very little in savings to pick up the slack, had been stressful on a lot of levels.

She inserted the memory stick into one of the USB ports and crossed her fingers that several months in a jar of peach preserves hadn't done any damage.

A message informed her the flash drive was loading its own software onto the computer, and a moment later the drive appeared on the list of drives. "Let's see what we have."

As she'd suspected, the flash drive was full of photographs. Over two hundred total. There was only one text file on the entire drive. It was titled "ForBR."

"This is for me," she said, surprised.

"Open it," Dalton said.

She double-clicked the file and held her breath. A short

note popped up. "Briar, if you ever find this, it means things went bad. I know you won't like what I've done, but I did it for Logan. He deserves more than we got growing up. But if you're reading this, I'm probably dead anyway. So do what you want with it."

Dalton's hand slid up to her neck, gently kneading the tight muscles bunched there. "Eloquent." His dry tone left little doubt about his assessment of Johnny's character.

Briar couldn't blame him, really. Johnny had been a very flawed man. She didn't try to defend him.

"You want to see what's on these files?" Dalton asked.

"Let's copy them to the computer first." She pulled up a second window, made a new folder she named JB and started the files copying to the hard drive. The computer was old and slow, and her attempt to access any of the files while they were copying led to nothing but annoyance, as the image program displayed not the expected photograph but a spinning digital hourglass that seemed to taunt Briar as the seconds ticked into minutes.

Giving in to her rising frustration, she stood and crossed impatiently to the window looking out on the small side yard, wondering if the faint glow of the computer had caught the attention of anyone who might be staking out the cabin. She pulled the curtain back a scant inch and peered into the darkness.

"See anyone?" Dalton asked.

"No, but they're out there." She let the curtain slide back in place and turned back to look at him. In the faint blue glow of the computer screen, he looked tired and troubled. She knew if she were in his place, the thought of being tricked into letting an enemy into her own home would have been a constant gnawing ache in her soul.

What she couldn't figure out was why she wasn't angrier at him. Thanks to his incautious moment, her son was missing and in grave danger, and most of the way home from Virginia, she'd cursed Dalton's name and planned ways to make him regret his mistake. But by the time she'd arrived at his house and walked through the door to see him sitting there on the sofa looking sick and broken, all her anger had changed course and flowed toward the nameless, faceless person who'd betrayed his trust and left him looking so crushed and heartbroken.

And toward Blake Culpepper, of course, whose wicked greed and ruthlessness had made Logan a target in the first place.

A soft thudding sound from the front of the house drew her attention away from Dalton's pale face. He turned in his chair, as well, his gaze going toward the bedroom door.

"Stay here. Keep that thing copying."

"It'll copy without me," he said, falling in step as she reached the hallway. "Are you armed?"

"Of course. You?"

"Of course not," he said with a grimace.

She stepped back into the bedroom and unlocked the closet door. The Mossberg shotgun felt like an old friend in her grip. She grabbed some shells off the top shelf of the closet and loaded both barrels.

Back in the hallway, she pulled the Glock from her holster and handed it to Dalton. "Don't shoot if you don't have to. But if you do, go for center mass."

She edged her way down the hall, stopping just short of the front room. Holding her breath, she dared a quick look around the corner.

The front door was open.

She reached back, her palm connecting with Dalton's hip. She gave a little squeeze, holding him in place. "They're already inside," she whispered, her voice barely more than a breath.

He tensed beneath her touch, but he didn't flinch or edge back. He was in this thing till the end, she realized. Warmth flooded her body, as if the knowledge that Dalton would have her back was enough to quell the anxiety of facing a darkened room full of God only knew how many ruthless, dangerous men Blake had sent to bring her in.

Blake can't win, she thought, and for a moment she believed it.

Then all hell broke loose.

THE TWO CAMOUFLAGE-CLAD men entered the cabin just as Nix, Dana and Doyle reached the edge of the tree line. Doyle and Dana both appeared inclined to rush in after them, but Nix caught them both by their arms. "Wait a minute."

"They've just committed a crime. We have cause to take them in," Doyle growled.

"Someone's already in there," he said quietly. He'd spotted the slightest twitch of a curtain in Briar's bedroom window, barely visible through the trees as they'd made a stealthy approach through the woods. There was also an odd glow to the room, as if someone had turned on a television or something like it inside.

"Who?"

"If I were a betting man, I'd say it's Briar. And your brother's probably with her, too."

"Her car isn't anywhere around," Dana protested.

"So she walked. Or she had another way of getting here." Nix couldn't give them a more concrete reason for what was essentially one of his infamous hunches. He'd been teased about his intuition for years, mostly by well-meaning folks on the police force who got a kick of having a real-life Cherokee "seer" among them.

There wasn't anything paranormal about his hunches,

of course. He just paid attention to things like twitching curtains and glowing rooms.

Before Doyle or Dana had a chance to respond, a flurried sound of movement drifted out of the open cabin door, and Nix could no more have stopped Dana and Doyle from rushing toward the cabin than he could stop himself.

Outracing his fiancée and her brother to the porch, he took a leap up the three shallow steps and hit the wooden slats of the porch just as a shotgun blasted from somewhere inside the house. He ducked and rolled toward the side of the porch, crouching in a tight ball. Doyle and Dana, he saw, scattered in opposite directions, away from the open door.

"Anybody moves again, this time I aim for flesh. Got me?"

That was Briar's voice, Nix realized with an emotion that fluttered between alarm and relief.

A male voice followed, deep and thick with a mountain accent that turned his string of curses into a profane sort of music. But the gist of his flood of expletives was that he understood her words and would do nothing to invite her further wrath.

Nix couldn't hold back a grin.

"BILLY HACKMORE AND Terry McDavid." A thick rime of contempt crusted Briar's voice as she looked down at the two men Walker Nix and Doyle Massey had just subdued and cuffed. Dalton wondered if she should put down the shotgun now, but he didn't want to be the one to ask her to do so.

"Boys, at the very least, we have you on breaking and entering. Plus, we're going to run your names, see if there are any outstanding warrants. And whether or not you have the right paperwork for these weapons." Doyle waved his hand toward the four pistols lying on the nearby kitchen table. "Seein' as how they all seem to have the serial numbers filed off, I'm thinkin' that might be an issue."

Dalton glanced at his brother. After just a few short months in Bitterwood, Doyle was already losing his flatlander accent and beginning to pick up a mountain twang. His beach tan was also fading. He'd be a mountain man in no time.

Oddly, Dalton was starting to think of himself as a mountain man, as well. The thought of leaving these hills behind didn't hold nearly as much charm as it once had.

All the charms he could want in the world, he thought as he watched Briar lower her shotgun and shake her rowdy curls back from her face, seemed to be located right here in the Smoky Mountains.

"I'm thinking you don't have any reason to be loyal to Blake Culpepper beyond the money he tosses your way. Or maybe you're afraid of him?" At the flicker of fear in both men's eyes, Doyle leaned a little closer, taking advantage of his own power, both physical and legal, to keep the two captives off guard. "You should be afraid of me instead."

"Where is Blake?" Briar had apparently reached the end of her patience. She charged closer, making Terry McDavid, who sat nearest her, flinch away.

Dalton caught her arm. She whirled on him, and the ferocity of her gaze nearly made him recoil, as well. With obvious effort, she regained control of her anger.

"It's a good question," Doyle agreed far more calmly. "Where is Blake Culpepper? Where is he keeping Logan?"

"He'll kill us if we tell you," Billy Hackmore said.

"And I'll make you wish you were dead if you don't," Briar growled.

Doyle gave her a pointed look and she growled again but turned away, stalking out through the open front door.

Dalton followed her out, easing his arms around her. She quivered like a wild animal that had been cornered, but after a moment she gentled beneath his touch, leaning back against him. He tightened his embrace, burying his face in her curls. "They don't owe Culpepper any loyalty," he murmured. "Doyle will break one of them sooner or later."

"The longer Logan stays with Blake, the more likely something terrible will happen to him." A nervous ripple ran through her slender body, and he hugged her tighter. "And even if we find out where he is, what next? A SWAT raid? With my baby as a hostage?"

"We'll figure something out," he said, although he wasn't sure how to avoid just the scenario she imagined. Blake Culpepper was almost certainly well armed. Getting inside and getting Logan out wasn't going to be easy.

"I have to go alone," she murmured.

His body stiffened reflexively. "And give him two hostages?"

She turned in his arms, looking up at him in the glow spilling from inside the cabin. Dark shadows of anxiety bruised the flesh around her stormy eyes. "I'm not so easy to take hostage."

Her skin looked like velvet. He couldn't resist the urge to touch her cheek, to see if it was as soft as it looked. He brushed the pad of his thumb over her lips, and they parted, her soft breath warming his hand. "I want Logan back with us. More than anything. But I don't want to sacrifice you to make it happen. There's got to be a way that doesn't put you in that man's hands."

Her gaze met his, direct and unflinching. "I don't think there is. So I have to know—will you back me on this? Or do you plan to fight me?"

The thought of Briar going into Culpepper's lair, unarmed and alone, was unthinkable. And yet he knew she was asking him to not only think it but support her decision.

She wanted him to trust her instincts, to believe that she knew what she was doing and could bring her son home safely. And, God help him, he couldn't refuse anything she asked. Not even this.

"Okay. I'll back you. But I want to be there with you."

She shook her head sharply. "No."

"I won't go in with you. I'll let you play it however you want. But I'm going to be outside whatever lair your cousin's holed up in. No way in hell do I let you walk in there without backup. Are you going to back me on that? Or do you plan to fight me?"

She stared up at him, the look in her eyes a mixture of consternation and affection as she recognized her own words thrown back at her. "You're a lawyer, you know. You can't even shoot a rifle worth a damn."

"You're good for a man's self-esteem, Briar. Anyone ever tell you that?"

A bleak look passed over her face, and he realized he'd touched a nerve.

Tugging her closer, he bent and whispered in her ear. "You make me want to be a better man. You make me believe it's possible."

Her eyes flickered up to meet his as he backed away. One small work-roughened hand rose to his face, her thumb sliding over his lips the way he'd touched hers. "When this is over…"

He silenced her with a soft kiss.

The sound of a throat clearing drew them apart. They both looked toward the doorway, where Nix stood, his expression bemused. "We have a location."

Chapter Sixteen

"I wish we had time to wire you," Doyle grumbled as he looked from his brother to Briar. "But you're right. We need to move fast, before he's had time to wonder why his men aren't reporting back."

"What about those two?" Dalton nodded toward the two men in cuffs.

"Dana and Nix will stay with them. We're not going to call this in to the station until we have a chance to get Logan away from Culpepper," Doyle answered. Unspoken in his reply was the unsettling knowledge that they still weren't sure who in the police station could be trusted.

"There's a copy of this disk on the computer in my bedroom," Briar said quietly. "Maybe, if these files are what we think they are, they'll be able to tell you a lot more about who's a friend and who's not."

"I need a weapon," Dalton said.

Briar handed him the Glock he'd returned to her earlier at the house. She wasn't going to need it in the cabin on Smoky Ridge where Blake was holed up with her son. "Fifteen rounds, plus one in the chamber."

He nodded, looking both worried and determined. If she hadn't already been more than halfway in love with him, she'd have loved him a little just for backing her up on this risky plan. She knew she was asking a lot of him.

Of all of them. She was asking them to put their trust in her to handle herself in a battle of wills with one of the most dangerous men in the Smoky Mountains, with her son's life at stake.

"Dalton and I will come with you up to the cabin. Then we'll wait."

"We can't wire her up," Dalton murmured, "but what if we listen in through her cell phone?"

"He may take my phone as soon as I enter the cabin," she warned.

"And he may not. But even if he does, your phone display can go black even when a call is connected, right?"

She nodded, understanding his point. "And he may not think to check if it's on."

"Good idea," Doyle said. The look of pleasure on Dalton's face at his brother's approval would have been comical if it weren't so poignant. Briar had a feeling Tallie Cumberland's children were going to end up being a family after all.

Blake Culpepper's choice of hideouts was pretty brilliant, Briar had to concede as she led Dalton and Doyle through the thickening woods. The cabin was the old Cumberland homestead, abandoned years earlier when the inhabitants of Cherokee Cove had driven the accursed family from their midst after Tallie Cumberland's troubles with the Sutherlands and Hales. It was the one place in Cherokee Cove that nobody would ever think to go, for fear of the curse rubbing off on them.

The place was secluded but not particularly primitive. It had indoor plumbing and electricity. Briar assumed, as they came within sight of the mountain cabin, Blake had probably figured out a way to pirate the electricity that now lit up a room in the back of the small wooden structure. He was hardly a man who'd blink at such an easy bit of theft.

She paused and turned to her companions. Doyle was looking through narrowed eyes at the cabin, but Dalton's gaze was firmly on her. She felt an odd little thrill at being his singular focus at this peril-fraught moment.

"Be careful," he said, and there was a wealth of unspoken emotion behind his words. She felt an answering flood of feeling building like a fire in the center of her chest.

She pulled out her cell phone. "Your phone's on vibrate?"

He nodded.

She dialed his number. His cell phone buzzed. He swiped the screen and she lifted her phone to her ear, locking gazes with him as she spoke softly into the phone. "Let's bring Logan home."

His eyes glittered as he nodded. "Don't stop talking. If you stop talking, I might be tempted to come in and get you."

"If I stop talking, go in there and get my boy." She reached across the narrow space between them, touching her hand to his chest. "Promise me."

"I promise."

Doyle touched her shoulder. "We both promise. Take care." He nodded toward the cabin.

Her heart pounding like thunder, she walked slowly into the clearing.

Half expecting to be cut down by bullets before she reached the porch, she was surprised to make it all the way to the cabin's front door without incident. But she wasn't shocked when the door whipped open before she could lift her hand to knock and the double barrels of a shotgun greeted her.

Blake Culpepper stood behind the shotgun, his dark eyes narrow with suspicion. "Son of a bitch," he muttered with disgust. "I should have known not to send a couple of idiots to grab another Culpepper."

"I'm a Blackwood," she answered tartly, quelling the quiver of fear rattling through her. "That's really why you went after me, isn't it? Because of what Johnny took?"

He gave the shotgun a sideways twitch and backed up a few feet. Briar took the gesture as all the invitation she was going to get. Moving slowly, she entered the cabin, barely suppressing a flinch as the door shut behind her, slammed in place by one sharp kick of Blake's boot.

"Where is my son?" She lifted her chin and met her cousin's gaze.

His eyes glittered with almost indulgent amusement, as if he were watching a fluffy kitten show its tiny claws. *Good,* she thought. *Keep thinking I'm harmless.*

"Where are the files?" he countered.

She reached for the flash drive in the front pocket of her jeans. He jerked the barrel of the shotgun toward her. "Uh-uh."

Pressing her lips flat with revulsion, she stood still while he moved his hands over her body, looking for any sign of a weapon. She was clean, of course; she'd brought with her only her cell phone and the flash drive. Even her pocketknife was stashed in the pocket of Dalton's jacket.

As they'd hoped, Blake didn't bother checking to see if the phone was engaged. He shoved it back at her, and she slipped it back into the pocket of her windbreaker. He kept the flash drive, looking at it through narrowed eyes. For a moment the barrel of the shotgun dipped away from her, and she gauged her chance of overpowering him.

Not good, she decided. And too early. She couldn't be sure Blake had her son here in this cabin, despite the assurances of his henchmen back at her cabin. She needed to see Logan, make sure he was safe, before she took any risky chances.

"You have the files," she said. "Where is Logan?"

"I have a memory stick," he said bluntly, bringing up the barrel of the shotgun again. "Could be pictures of your Dollywood trip, for all I know."

"Never been to Dollywood," she answered. "Always wanted to, but money being short—"

He answered with another sideways twitch of the gun. "The kid's back here." He waited for her to move toward the doorway leading to the back of the cabin, then followed, the barrel of the shotgun flattening against her spine, right between her shoulder blades.

Right where her heart was hammering like a carpenter on speed.

"Mama!" Logan's voice, coming over the cell phone with tinny clarity, made Dalton's whole body rattle with relief. He looked up at Doyle, who grinned back at him as Briar's phone crooned endearments to her son. There was a soft swishing sound over the phone—Briar sweeping her little boy into her arms and hugging him tight?

It's what Dalton would have done in the same situation.

"Why don't you and your boy catch up while I take a look at these files?" Blake Culpepper's gravelly voice sounded sly through the phone. He was up to something, Dalton thought with a flutter of alarm. Could Briar hear it, too?

"Why don't we come up front with you instead?" she asked.

"You really don't take this shotgun seriously, do you?"

"I take it very seriously," she countered, sounding confident and calm. She was, Dalton thought, an utterly remarkable woman. He didn't deserve a woman like that in his life, but he'd be damned if he didn't try to keep her there anyway.

"Ah, hell. Why not? You've probably made copies of it already, haven't you?" Blake sounded more resigned than annoyed, making Dalton wonder if he had been right about why Blake wanted his hands on the files. If he planned to use them to eliminate his competition, it probably didn't matter much to him if the police brought in his foes and saved him some of the trouble.

"You think you can avoid capture, don't you?" Briar's tone sounded more conversational than confrontational.

"Ain't nobody knows these woods better than a Culpepper, darlin'. You know that better than most."

She didn't argue. Over the phone, Dalton heard the sound of footsteps as well as the soft murmur of Logan's little-boy voice saying something Dalton couldn't quite make out. Briar's answer was a soft shushing sound, a mother trying to keep her son from drawing unwanted attention.

"Stay right here, Logan. Stay close to Mama." Dalton heard the soft thud of feet shuffling on the floor. Had she set the little boy down? He wondered why she'd let him go instead of holding on tight.

He didn't like the answer that came to mind.

"Let's see what's on these files," Blake said. The faint sound of metal scraping metal drifted over the phone line. Dalton tried to picture what was happening in the cabin, but all his mind seemed able to focus on was why Briar had set her son down instead of holding him close.

What was she planning?

BRIAR SLOWLY BENT her knees, easing into a crouch next to her son as Blake pulled up a metal folding chair to the table where a laptop computer sat open, its screen dark.

He had settled himself where he could see her, but he'd leaned the shotgun against the wall beside him, as if he no longer considered her much of a threat.

Big mistake, she thought with rising confidence.

But she still had to be careful. Logan could easily get hurt if she tried to overpower Blake and take away the shotgun. She couldn't move yet. Not while Logan was in the room.

She hugged Logan close, nuzzling his neck. He was sweaty and a little grimy, but he still smelled like heaven to her. "How you doin', little man?" she murmured in his ear, glancing at Blake to see if he was listening.

His attention was focused on the files now opening on the laptop.

"He didn't hurt you, did he?"

Blake didn't react, but Logan answered, "He yells."

Blazing fury shot up her gullet and filled her throat with rage. She tamped it down and glanced at Blake again.

"Logan," she whispered, "when I say go, I want you to run out the door, okay? Just nod."

Logan nodded solemnly.

She glanced at Blake again. He was smiling at the laptop screen as he pulled up photo after photo. "Gotta hand it to Johnny," he said. "He was thorough."

"How did you know he had the files?" She pushed to a standing position and edged sideways, putting Logan firmly behind her.

Blake looked up at her briefly. "He tried to sell them to Merritt Cortland. He'd heard tell Merritt was trying to undercut old man Cortland. I guess he thought Merritt would be willing to shell out a few bucks to get his hands on the files."

Her heart sank a little. So much for Johnny's intentions being honorable. "Merritt wasn't buying?"

Blake shrugged, turning back to the computer. "Merritt made the mistake of thinking Johnny had the files on him. He stabbed first and asked questions later. Too much later."

Her blood ran cold. Blake was talking about Johnny's murder with as little feeling as if he'd been discussing putting poison on an anthill. Briar may have fallen out of love with her husband by the time he was murdered, but he'd been her first love and the father of her son. To hear his murder discussed with such heartless dispassion made her want to grab the shotgun and start shooting things.

She managed to remain motionless, her gaze firmly on Blake's profile. She studied him, looking for an opening.

He opened another file, and his eyes widened. He murmured a string of profanities, leaning closer to the computer.

Now, she thought.

She reached behind her and touched Logan's head. "Go!"

She heard his little feet pattering toward the door. Blake was slow to react, but when he realized what was happening, he reached for the shotgun.

She launched herself at him, her shoulder slamming into the barrel of the shotgun before it swung around to face her. With a deafening blast, the shotgun went off.

Two things happened in quick succession. First, the door of the cabin opened and Logan Blackwood came running out, his tiny legs churning.

And second, a shotgun blast split the silence of the deepening night.

Dalton and Doyle moved at the same time, brushing shoulders briefly as they ran. By the time they reached the cabin steps, Logan had made his way down them. With a glance at his brother, Dalton churned his way past the little boy and up the steps, leaving Doyle to scoop up the boy and run him back to safety.

Dalton faltered to a stop in the cabin doorway. Briar and Blake were standing upright but twisted around each other as they grappled, the shotgun perilously clutched between them. Though Blake was larger than Briar by at least seventy pounds and six inches, she had a mother's fierceness on her side, and she was close to taking him down to the ground.

But the shotgun was too close to her face. Only one blast had sounded, and the weapon had two barrels.

She'd told him to shoot for center mass, but her center mass was too damned close to Culpepper's. So he did the only thing he knew to do. He walked up boldly behind Blake and pressed the gun to the back of the man's neck. "I will kill you," he said in a tone so calm and emotionless that he almost didn't recognize his own voice.

Blake froze in place. But Briar didn't. Jerking the shotgun from his loosening grip, she slammed the butt of the gun right in her cousin's gut.

Air whooshed from Blake's chest, and he sagged backward, nearly toppling Dalton to the floor. Dalton braced his legs and kept the pistol pointed at the man's head as he struggled to keep Blake on his feet.

"Let him go," Briar demanded. She'd shifted the shotgun into shooting position, the barrel aimed squarely at her cousin's midsection.

"Put it down," Dalton said, alarm crawling up his spine at the look of sheer feral rage in her thundercloud eyes.

She shook her head, her gaze pinned to Blake's face. "Is Merritt Cortland still alive?" she asked through gritted teeth.

Blake made a groaning sound, still trying to suck in air.

"Is that bastard still alive?" Briar demanded, pushing the barrel of the shotgun right up to Blake's chest.

"Briar, put down the shotgun," Dalton said. "If you shoot him, you'll shoot me."

Her gaze flickered up to meet his, and some of the fire he saw burning behind her eyes cooled to just a flicker. She released a long, gusty breath, pain lining her features. "Merritt Cortland murdered Johnny."

"I know. I heard."

Her face started to crumple, and she backed away, lowering the shotgun barrel. With shaking hand, she pulled her cell phone from her pocket, pushed a couple of buttons and lifted the phone to her ear. "Chief? We could use a little help."

Chapter Seventeen

"This information is explosive." Tom Bevill's voice was usually enough to make Dalton snap to attention, but he couldn't seem to drag his gaze away from Briar's pale face. She sat across the police station foyer from him, rocking her sleeping son in her lap. Her gray-eyed gaze was distant and unfocused, making him wonder what she was thinking.

"Are you listening to me, Dalton?"

Dalton looked at his boss. "The files were all we hoped for?"

"And more. We have names, events—it's a treasure trove of actionable evidence as well as new threads for future investigations." Bevill's smile was almost wistful. "Makes me want to rethink my plans to retire."

"You should," Dalton said. "Rethink it, I mean."

Bevill's eyes narrowed. "You want me to run against you?"

"I'm not running," he said, giving voice to something he'd been thinking about off and on for the past couple of days.

Bevill looked stunned. "You've been planning to run for my job since you first signed on with the prosecutor's office. What happened?"

Dalton's gaze wandered back to Briar and her son. "I'm

thinking of making changes in my life. I don't need to add an election to that mix."

"I always figured you'd end up in the governor's office one day. Hell, maybe even the White House in time."

That would never happen, Dalton thought, thanks to his family's scandals. But he'd come to realize the dream of political service had always been more important to his father and grandfather than it had been to him. He liked being a prosecutor, finding justice for people who'd been wronged. And he hated politics. "I like the work I'm doing now."

Bevill's eyes narrowed, but he simply nodded. "I guess I should make an announcement canceling my plans for retirement. Maybe I'll announce it at this morning's press conference. You'll be there? Give me your support?"

"Sure." Dalton supposed there was no way to avoid politics altogether in his line of work.

"Good man." Bevill clapped his shoulder. "We'll be meeting in a couple of hours to plan the press conference about this bust. You'll be there, too?"

In any other circumstances, he'd say yes, despite feeling as if a whole beach's worth of sand had set up gritty shop in his eyes. But he had other matters he needed to deal with first. More important, even, than a press conference announcing a major arrest.

"The police want me to stick around a little while longer," he told his boss. At least, he hoped one particular police officer wanted him to stick around for a lot longer.

But his hope of talking to Briar alone anytime soon evaporated even as Tom Bevill headed off in search of a phone. Walker Nix had taken a seat next to Briar, his head close to hers in tense conversation.

Dalton crossed to where they sat. "Has something happened?"

Nix looked up. "We finally reached the gate guard who was on duty this morning. We've identified who visited you." The man's look of sympathy made Dalton's gut tighten.

"Who?" he asked.

Briar touched his arm. "It was Janet."

He stared at her a moment. "Janet Trainor? My secretary Janet?"

Nix nodded. "She signed in with a false name, but the gate guard's description was clear and detailed. On a hunch, Doyle called Laney and gave her the description. She said it sounded just like Janet Trainor."

Dalton felt sick. "Janet's been with me for years. She's a good woman. I would have trusted her with any of my secrets."

"She's been picked up for questioning. We're about to talk to her. If you'd like to observe the interview, we can arrange it."

He nodded. "I'd like to hear what she has to say."

He half hoped Briar would come with him, but while her hand tightened around his arm before he rose from his chair, she remained where she was. Swallowing a sigh of disappointment, he went with Nix through the detective's office and into Doyle's corner lair.

Doyle was there already, along with Laney and Dana. Sympathy shined in all three pairs of eyes. "Nix briefed you?" Doyle asked.

"Yeah. Who's doing the interview?"

"Delilah Brand," Doyle answered. "She and Janet were schoolmates back in the day."

They'd set up the chief's laptop computer to pick up the feed from the interview room. The picture was a little grainy, but the audio was clean. The tremble in Janet Trainor's voice came through loud and clear.

"You know, don't you?" she said before Delilah asked the first question.

"What do you think we know?" Delilah asked.

Janet began to cry, tears trickling down her pale cheeks. "Please, you have to understand—if they find out you know, they'll kill him."

Dalton leaned toward the screen.

"Kill who?" Dana murmured a second before Delilah asked the same thing in the interview room.

"Hunter," Janet answered in a soft whimper.

"Who's Hunter?" Doyle asked.

"Her brother," Dalton answered, the situation beginning to make a terrible sort of sense. "Hunter Bragg. Former Army infantry soldier. He was injured in an IED explosion in Afghanistan about a year ago. Army deemed him unfit for retention, and apparently he's pretty depressed about it."

"She's been worried about him," Laney said quietly. "Everybody knows how she worries about him."

"Who's going to kill him?" Delilah asked Janet in a gentle tone.

"Blake Culpepper." Janet took the tissue Delilah offered her, wiping her eyes. Her voice was a little stronger now, as if admitting her fear had given back the strength her secret had stolen. "I got a message this morning at the office. It was waiting for me in my chair. It said there was a bottle in my desk drawer. The one I keep locked. The note told me they'd been watching Hunter and that if I didn't do what they told me to do with the contents of that bottle, they would kill him before I could reach him. There was a photo—"

"Do you have the note and the photo?"

Janet nodded unhappily. "I locked it in the glove compartment of my car."

"Get me a search warrant for that car," Doyle said.

Nix nodded and headed out of the office.

"What did the photo show?" Delilah asked.

"Hunter. Tied up and gagged. They will kill him if they know I'm here."

Doyle gave Dalton a troubled look. "Blake Culpepper has already invoked his Fifth Amendment rights. He's law-yered up. He won't talk."

"Ask her for permission to see the photo. Tell her we have Culpepper in custody and we need to try to find her brother," Dalton said. "She'll cooperate."

Before Doyle could move, Delilah did just that. "We can get a search warrant for your car, but if you'll give us permission—"

"Of course," Janet said quickly. "Anything."

Dalton turned away from the computer screen, his gut roiling. Janet must have come by his house on some pre-text. He'd have let her in, without a doubt. Maybe he'd made them some coffee and she'd slipped the GHB into his cup, as ordered.

Good God, he thought, *the poor woman.*

"I wanted to call the police," she was saying, her voice clear over the computer. "Please tell me that Dalton's okay. Please, please tell me that."

"He's okay," Delilah said.

No, Dalton thought as he walked out of the office, *he's not. Dalton is definitely not okay.*

Briar realized she was being overly cautious, clinging to her son instead of letting someone find him a soft sofa somewhere in the cop shop to finish off his slumber. She just didn't want to let him go yet.

But when Dana came downstairs with news of a wrinkle

in their formerly wrapped-up case, she realized she had to put her cop hat back on and let someone else watch her son.

Blake wouldn't be coming after him now. There was nothing he needed from her anymore.

"Laney's agreed to watch him," Dana told her, the look in her green eyes full of apology. "I know it's too soon, but you and Nix know Cherokee Cove better than anyone else. He wants you in on this investigation. Time could be running out for Hunter Bragg."

Briar felt as if she'd been run over by a fleet of trucks, but one look at the photo Nix had found in Janet Trainor's car gave her a double shot of refreshed energy. The man in the photo still bore the scars of his war injury, along with new scrapes and bruises he'd no doubt earned during his more recent capture.

The thought of Blake Culpepper's band of ruthless thieves and killers using a war hero as leverage against a decent woman almost made her wish she'd blasted a hole in her cousin the way she'd wanted to back in his cabin.

She dragged her gaze away from the battered face and focused instead on the background of the photo, trying to figure out if anything looked familiar. "It looks like a cabin, not a house," she said after a moment. "There's something…" She paused, peering a little closer at the grainy out-of-focus background of the photograph. Her stomach gave a small lurch as she realized what it was. "See that black blur there, behind his shoulder?"

Dana nodded. "Can you tell what it is?"

She could be wrong, but if she was right—

If she was right, she realized with a sinking heart, then a whole lot of what she'd assumed about the world around her could be dead wrong.

"I think," she said finally, reluctantly, "it might be a black-bear skin."

"Does that mean anything?" Dana asked.

"I think it does." Her stomach knotting, she pushed to her feet. Logan shifted in her arms, clinging a little more tightly to her neck even in his sleep. The urge to keep him wrapped in her arms forever was so strong she almost sat back down. But the image of that bound and gagged soldier gave her the strength to keep going. She was beginning to believe she knew exactly where she'd seen that bearskin before, as much as she wanted to believe otherwise. And if she was right, Hunter Bragg was in a hell of a lot of danger.

They all were.

"Do you know where Dalton is?" she asked Dana as they hurried through the empty corridor toward the detectives' communal office.

"He was in Doyle's office with us watching the interview with Janet Trainor earlier," Dana answered. "You can imagine how shocked he was to learn who'd drugged him and took Logan."

"Is he still there?"

"No. He left the office after learning why Janet had drugged him. I don't even know if he's still here in the station."

Damn. She really wanted to see him before she left. Ask him, maybe, to stay with Laney and make sure Logan was okay. But she didn't have time to hunt him down. Hunter Bragg might be in a hell of a lot of trouble, even more than they thought.

"If you see Dalton, will you tell him where I went?" She wasn't sure he was in any hurry to talk to her, given how close she'd come to blowing him away along with her cousin earlier that night, but she needed to try, at least, to explain. To find out if it was possible to get past all of the craziness of the past few days and see if the attraction between them had any legs.

For her, she knew, it did. She'd been in love before. She knew what it felt like. And if she wasn't already there with Dalton, it wouldn't take much to get her to that point.

She just needed to know if she was fooling herself. Could he ever feel that way about her, too? Could they get past the obvious differences in their lives, in their pasts, and build something good and lasting for the future?

DALTON STARED AT his sister in dismay. "She's going on a raid?"

"Nix wanted her with him," she said flatly.

Nix, he thought with a grimace. "Your boyfriend does realize she's been awake for nearly twenty-four hours and she has a little boy who needs her with him?"

"She agreed to go," Dana answered, clearly trying not to bristle at his tone when he spoke of her fiancé. "She knows the area better than anyone but Nix. And there's a man's life at stake. A war hero, for God's sake."

Dalton rubbed his hand over his gritty eyes. "Have they located where he's being held?"

"Nix just called in with an affirmative. Doyle's about to send backup before they try to go in and get him."

"Who has him?"

"They haven't told me," she admitted. "I get the feeling it's a situational security thing. They don't want to be overheard."

Odd, he thought. Then again, the police station had been the locus of a recent not-quite-completed corruption investigation. "Have they left yet?"

Dana shook her head. "They're gearing up now. Why?"

Dalton started moving toward the police station's weapons-and-gear lockers, leaving her to catch up. "Because I'm going with them."

NIX'S DARK EYES bored into Briar's from the back corner of the mountain cabin. He nodded twice. The signal to go.

She was the only one not wearing protective gear, though her Glock was snugly tucked into a pancake holster snapped to the back of her jeans. She hadn't bothered freshening up before leaving the station. The more her weariness and strain showed, the better.

She rounded the corner of the cabin and climbed the porch steps, not bothering to be quiet. She wasn't there in stealth mode, after all.

She was the distraction.

The front door was made of solid pine slabs stained to a dark oak color. Knocking three times, she braced herself for whatever came next. It took a lot of control not to reach behind her to check on the presence of the Glock, but her job was to appear as normal and nonthreatening as a police officer could manage.

The door opened a few inches, making her nerves jangle all the way to her toes. She struggled not to show it, struggled not to react to the face she saw staring back at her in the open doorway, even though nausea rippled through her at the familiar sight.

"Good God, Blackwood," Thurman Gowdy growled, his voice gravelly with sleep. "Do you realize it's four in the morning?"

"Can I come in?" she asked.

Her patrol partner peered at her through narrowed eyes. His salt-and-pepper crew cut managed to look mussed despite its short, crisp length, as if he'd just rolled out of bed. Maybe he had, she thought. He had no reason to think his cabin was about to be raided. He probably didn't even know Blake was in custody yet.

"What's happened?" he asked.

"Logan was kidnapped," she answered, phrasing it so

she didn't give away whether or not he was still missing. Just in case she was wrong and he had already heard the news.

"I know. I'm so sorry." He looked so sincere, she thought, her stomach cramping with dismay. "I asked if I could be in on the hunt for him, but they said at the station they were trying to go low profile on it. Is there anything new on it?"

She wasn't sure if he didn't know or if he knew and was trying to trap her. Her weary mind couldn't figure out his meaning, so she just got to the point of her visit.

"Can I come in?" she repeated.

He hesitated, and the last of her doubts disappeared, leaving only disillusionment coiling like a snake in her chest. If Hunter Bragg weren't hidden somewhere in the cabin, her partner would have let her in without a thought.

"My brother's here, and he's a light sleeper," Thurman said. "Maybe I could meet you in a few minutes at Ledbetter's for some coffee and an early breakfast?" He glanced back toward the darkness behind him.

It gave her the distraction she needed.

She whipped the Glock from her holster. By the time he turned back around to face her, the pistol was pointed straight at his chest.

The shock on his face was real, she realized. "Good God, Blackwood, what are you doing?"

"Is there anyone in your cabin besides your prisoner?" she asked.

He feigned confusion. "Prisoner? What the hell are you talking about? Put down the gun, Blackwood. Have you lost your mind?"

She felt more than heard Nix coming up the porch steps behind her. "It's over, Gowdy. You made a mistake when you took that picture of Hunter Bragg. You forgot to move the bearskin off the wall behind him."

Thurman's expression shifted to dismay. Slowly, he raised his hands and twined them behind the back of his head. "I want a lawyer."

"Is there anyone in the cabin besides Bragg?" she asked.

Gowdy just stared at her, silent.

Nix led two deputies from the county sheriff's department's SWAT team into the cabin. Briar kept her weapon trained on Gowdy, lowering it only when Delilah Brand and another Ridge County deputy took him into custody. "Good work, Briar," Delilah said, sparing her a brief sympathetic smile.

She lowered her gun, trying to squelch the urge to sit in the nearby porch rocker and cry like a baby.

"He's here," Nix's voice called from the back of the cabin. "He's safe."

More deputies moved past her into the house. She didn't follow, instead trudging slowly down the porch steps and out toward the tree line at the edge of the yard. Sunrise was still at least a couple of hours away, but a faint lightening in the eastern sky over the mountains eased enough of the darkness for her to make out the shapes of trees and bushes in the mist-draped woods.

Suddenly, someone glided out of the gloom to stand in front of her. Dalton Hale, her mind registered with numb surprise. She blinked her eyes a couple of times, expecting the sight to disappear like the fatigue-induced fantasy it must surely be.

But he didn't disappear. He moved closer through the gray predawn light, his gaze locked with hers. "Are you okay?" he asked.

She wanted to tell him she was fine. But she couldn't push the words past her aching throat.

His eyes softening, he opened his arms and waited.

She didn't mean to run, but she must have, for one second he was a couple of yards away and the next she was pressed tightly against his body, wrapped up in a fierce, comforting embrace.

"I'm sorry," he said. "I would never have suspected Thurman Gowdy of being part of this mess."

She rubbed her face against his shirt. "It makes me wonder who to trust." She leaned back her head to look at him. "I heard about Janet."

"I suppose I should feel a little betrayed by what she did. I guess you must be angry at her."

She was, she had to admit. At first. But the more the image of Hunter Bragg's battered face had dug its claws into her thoughts, the less she could blame Janet Trainor for making the only choice she could bear to make. "I don't think I could have made a different choice in her position," she said.

He nodded toward the cabin, where Nix and the sheriff's deputies were leading Hunter Bragg from the cabin. The man was hunched and shivering beneath a thick quilt, but he was limping along under his own power, Briar saw with relief. She looked back at Dalton, who was still watching the scene through narrowed eyes. "They'll call it in to the station if they haven't already. Someone will let Janet know her brother is okay."

"I don't know what's going to happen to her. She kidnapped your son and turned him over to a criminal. I don't think we can just make the charges against her go away." He dragged his gaze back to hers, his grim look softening as he added, "I called Laney a few minutes ago to check on Logan. She said he's fine. Still asleep on the sofa in Doyle's office. She says Doyle's taking his sentry job very seriously."

She smiled, latching on to the one unadulterated bit of good news in her life at the moment. "I heard before I left that the county prosecutor was thrilled with getting his hands on that flash drive."

"He definitely was." Dalton smiled back at her, though there was a hint of reticence in his expression, as if there was something he wasn't looking forward to telling her.

Her own smile faded, and her stomach began to knot again, nearly as badly as it had before, while she was waiting for her partner to answer the cabin door and crush her last stubborn bit of hope that she was wrong about him. "What's wrong?"

He looked surprised by the question. "Nothing's wrong."

She wasn't convinced. "Did Bevill say something to worry you?"

His surprise faded into resignation. "No, it's not my boss I'm worried about."

"He's still going to back you as his replacement, isn't he?" she asked. She couldn't imagine the county prosecutor holding all that had happened to Dalton in the past few weeks against him. He was still the same smart, passionate prosecutor he'd been before the truth about his family came out. And he'd certainly proved his courage and determination during the past few tumultuous days while protecting her and Logan. "If he's giving you trouble, I can talk to him. I can tell him how amazing you've been—"

He smiled, though the worry in his eyes didn't quite disappear. "He's thinking about running again."

She looked at him in dismay. "He can't do that!"

"He can," Dalton assured her. "In fact, I encouraged him to do so."

"Are you crazy? Do you know how hard it'll be to beat a popular incumbent?"

"I'm dropping out of the race."

Now she knew he was crazy. "Why? You can't think people are going to hold what your father and grandfather did against you! People are smart enough to know you're blameless—"

"I never wanted to be a politician," he told her, curving his hands over her shoulders. His thumbs brushed lightly over her collarbone through her thin cotton T-shirt, making her shiver. "I just want to help people get a little justice in this world. I'm not cut out for politics."

She wanted to tell him he was cut out for anything he wanted, but she could see by the relief in his eyes that he'd already figured out what he wanted, and it didn't include running for office.

But did it include her?

She screwed up her courage and opened her mouth to breach the topic. But before she could speak, he lifted one hand to her cheek, his touch gentle and questing. "What I want," he murmured in a voice that made her blood spontaneously ignite, "is you. You and Logan. I want to go to my office and do what I can to help people, then come home to you and the little man and do what I can to make you feel happy and secure." A hint of doubt flickered in his eyes. "Do you think that's possible? I know the past few days have been nothing but crazy, but there's something between us, Briar. I feel it so strongly—it's like you're in my blood and there's nothing I could ever do to get you out. And I don't want to. I don't want to ever lose the feeling that you're part of me. That we're supposed to be like this. Am I crazy?"

Tears burned her eyes, but she wouldn't let them fall. She wanted to be clear-eyed and levelheaded. She wanted to talk about the problems and the struggles they'd have if they wanted to blend their lives together long-term.

But when she opened her mouth, what came out was

not what she'd intended. "Yes," she said, unable to tamp down a bubble of joy that burst into a smile. "Yes, you're crazy. And apparently I'm crazy, too."

He began to laugh, the sound just short of hysterical. His hand flexed convulsively against her face before wrapping around the back of her neck and pulling her into a hard, stake-claiming kiss.

Several breathless moments later, he drew back to catch his breath, his green eyes glittering with almost feral excitement. "I'm pretty sure I'm in love with you," he warned. "And I don't fall in love. So if you don't intend for this thing between us to be a long-term thing, better say so now."

Relief and a curious sort of triumph burned through her. She smiled up at him, her confidence soaring. "How long is long-term?"

He shrugged, his gaze mirroring her own growing boldness. His lips curved with satisfaction and just a hint of cocky masculinity. "I don't know. I was thinking this might lead to…forever? Think you can handle that?"

"I'm a mountain girl," she said, rising on tiptoes to wrap her arms around his neck. "I can handle anything."

* * * * *

*Look for award-winning author Paula Graves's
brand-new miniseries,* THE GATES, *later in 2014.
You'll find it wherever
Harlequin Intrigue books are sold!*

#1491 SAWYER
The Lawmen of Silver Creek Ranch • by Delores Fossen

When FBI agent Sawyer Ryland's ex-lover, Cassidy O'Neal, shows up at his family's ranch with a newborn and a crazy story about kidnappers, Sawyer isn't sure what to believe. But he and Cassidy must untangle the secrets and lies and find their future.

#1492 THE DISTRICT
Brody Law • by Carol Ericson

When former lovers Eric Brody and Christina Sandoval follow a serial killer into the occult, their love may be the only weapon to stop the killer.

#1493 LAWLESS
Corcoran Team • by HelenKay Dimon

Hope Algier is unprepared to see her ex, undercover agent Joel Kidd. But when people around her start dying, she's smart enought to lean on the one man she knows can protect them all—Joel.

#1494 SCENE OF THE CRIME: RETURN TO MYSTIC LAKE
by Carla Cassidy

When FBI Agents Jackson Revannaugh and Marjorie Clinton join forces to solve a kidnapping, sparks fly and danger grows near, threatening not only their relationship but also their lives.

#1495 NAVY SEAL SURRENDER
Texas Family Reckoning • by Angi Morgan

Navy SEAL John Sloan must find high school sweetheart Alicia Adams's daughter to clear his estranged twin's name. Can he find the girl without losing his heart?

#1496 THE BODYGUARD
by Lena Diaz

Caroline Ashton has escaped her abusive society husband and hired bodyguard Luke Dawson to protect her from him. But when her husband is murdered, Luke must protect her from the police and a killer on the loose.

YOU CAN FIND MORE INFORMATION ON UPCOMING HARLEQUIN® TITLES, FREE EXCERPTS AND MORE AT WWW.HARLEQUIN.COM.

HICNM0414

REQUEST YOUR FREE BOOKS!
2 FREE NOVELS PLUS 2 FREE GIFTS!

⊞ HARLEQUIN®

INTRIGUE®

BREATHTAKING ROMANTIC SUSPENSE

YES! Please send me 2 FREE Harlequin Intrigue® novels and my 2 FREE gifts (gifts are worth about $10). After receiving them, if I don't wish to receive any more books, I can return the shipping statement marked "cancel." If I don't cancel, I will receive 6 brand-new novels every month and be billed just $4.74 per book in the U.S. or $5.24 per book in Canada. That's a savings of at least 14% off the cover price! It's quite a bargain! Shipping and handling is just 50¢ per book in the U.S. and 75¢ per book in Canada.* I understand that accepting the 2 free books and gifts places me under no obligation to buy anything. I can always return a shipment and cancel at any time. Even if I never buy another book, the two free books and gifts are mine to keep forever.

182/382 HDN F42N

Name	(PLEASE PRINT)	
Address		Apt. #
City	State/Prov.	Zip/Postal Code

Signature (if under 18, a parent or guardian must sign)

Mail to the **Harlequin® Reader Service:**
IN U.S.A.: P.O. Box 1867, Buffalo, NY 14240-1867
IN CANADA: P.O. Box 609, Fort Erie, Ontario L2A 5X3

**Are you a subscriber to Harlequin Intrigue books
and want to receive the larger-print edition?
Call 1-800-873-8635 or visit www.ReaderService.com.**

* Terms and prices subject to change without notice. Prices do not include applicable taxes. Sales tax applicable in N.Y. Canadian residents will be charged applicable taxes. Offer not valid in Quebec. This offer is limited to one order per household. Not valid for current subscribers to Harlequin Intrigue books. All orders subject to credit approval. Credit or debit balances in a customer's account(s) may be offset by any other outstanding balance owed by or to the customer. Please allow 4 to 6 weeks for delivery. Offer available while quantities last.

Your Privacy—The Harlequin® Reader Service is committed to protecting your privacy. Our Privacy Policy is available online at www.ReaderService.com or upon request from the Harlequin Reader Service.

We make a portion of our mailing list available to reputable third parties that offer products we believe may interest you. If you prefer that we not exchange your name with third parties, or if you wish to clarify or modify your communication preferences, please visit us at www.ReaderService.com/consumerschoice or write to us at Harlequin Reader Service Preference Service, P.O. Box 9062, Buffalo, NY 14269. Include your complete name and address.

HI13R

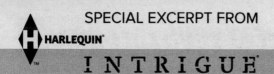
SAWYER
by USA TODAY *bestselling author*
Delores Fossen

A woman he'd spent one incredible night with and the baby who could be his will have Agent Sawyer Ryland fighting for a future he never imagined…

Agent Sawyer Ryland caught the movement from the corner of his eye, turned and saw the blonde pushing her way through the other guests who'd gathered for the wedding reception.

She wasn't hard to spot.

She was practically running, and she had a bundle of something gripped in front of her like a shield.

Sawyer's pulse kicked up a notch, and he automatically slid his hand inside his jacket and over his Glock. It was sad that his first response was to pull his firearm even at his own brother's wedding reception. Still, he'd been an FBI agent long enough—and had been shot too many times—that he lived by the code of better safe than sorry.

Or better safe than dead.

She stopped in the center of the barn that'd been decorated with hundreds of clear twinkling lights and flowers, and even though she was wearing dark sunglasses, Sawyer was pretty sure that her gaze rifled around. Obviously looking for someone. However, the looking around skidded to a halt when her attention landed on him.

"Sawyer," she said.

Because of the chattering guests and the fiddler sawing out some bluegrass, Sawyer didn't actually hear her speak his name. Instead, he saw it shape her trembling mouth. She yanked off the sunglasses, her gaze colliding with his.

"Cassidy O'Neal," he mumbled.

Yeah, it was her all right. Except she didn't much look like a pampered princess doll today in her jeans and body-swallowing gray T-shirt.

Despite the fact that he wasn't giving off any welcoming vibes whatsoever, Cassidy hurried to him. Her mouth was still trembling. Her dark green eyes rapidly blinking. There were beads of sweat on her forehead and upper lip despite the half dozen or so massive fans circulating air into the barn.

"I'm sorry," she said, and she thrust whatever she was carrying at him.

Sawyer didn't take it and backed up, but not before he caught a glimpse of the tiny hand gripping the white blanket.

A baby.

That put his heart right in his suddenly dry throat.

To find out what happens,
don't miss USA TODAY bestselling author
Delores Fossen's SAWYER, on sale in May 2014,
wherever Harlequin® Intrigue® books are sold!

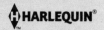

INTRIGUE®

IN THE CITY BY THE BAY, THE TRUTH WILL COME OUT...

A body left in the woods, marked by a killer... and it wasn't the first. The quicker Special Agent Christina Sandoval brought this serial killer to justice, the sooner she'd get back to her daughter. Reason enough for the FBI to have sent her partner...who was also her ex-fiancé, Eric Brody. While Brody's sense of justice never failed, his relationship with Sandoval had. The deeper they dug into the case, the more personal it got. With an elusive killer that seemed to know more about Christina than Brody ever did, they'd both need to stop holding back, or be the next to fall victim to this private war.

THE DISTRICT

BY CAROL ERICSON

Only from Harlequin® Intrigue®.
Available May 2014 wherever books are sold.

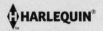

INTRIGUE

**WHEN A CORPORATE RETREAT TURNS
INTO CORPORATE SABOTAGE, THE
CORCORAN TEAM SENDS IN THEIR BEST**

Joel Kidd wasn't picked just for his risk assessment and
kidnap prevention skills. He had inside knowledge of the
mission's primaries: Hope Algier. Business had divided
the former lovers, and now that same dirty business
brought them back together. Touching down at this
high-end, out-of-the-way campground, Joel had the
perfect cover amongst these weekend warriors. In reality,
he was there to provide an extra layer of protection.
One Hope wouldn't accept, if she knew the truth. But
when an unknown assailant began picking off her clients
one by one, Joel was the only thing that could save them.
Though civilization—and safety—was still a long way off....

LAWLESS

by HELENKAY DIMON

*Only from Harlequin® Intrigue®.
Available May 2014 wherever books are sold.*